I0749175

Taos Vendetta

Also by James C. Wilson from Sunstone Press:

Hiking New Mexico's Chaco Canyon:
The Trails, The Ruins, The History

Santa Fe, City of Refuge:
An Improbable Memoir of the Counterculture

New Mexico's Chaco Canyon, Photographing the Ancient City

The Fernando Lopez Santa Fe Mystery Series:

Peyote Wolf
Smokescreen
Ghost Canyon
The Dead Go Fast
Painted Skull Ranch
Devil on Canyon Road
Taos Gothic

Taos Vendetta

A Fernando Lopez Santa Fe Mystery

James C. Wilson

Sunstone books may be purchased for educational, business, or sales promotional use.
For information please write: Special Markets Department, Sunstone Press,
P.O. Box 2321, Santa Fe, New Mexico 87504-2321.
Printed on acid-free paper
♾

Library of Congress Cataloging-in-Publication Data

Names: Wilson, James C., 1948- author. | Wilson, James C., 1948- Fernando Lopez Santa Fe mystery.
Title: Taos vendetta : a Fernando Lopez Santa Fe mystery / James C. Wilson.

Description: Santa Fe : Sunstone Press, [2023] | Series: A Fenando Lopez Santa Fe mystery | Summary: "The murder of a Hollywood actress sends private investigator Fernando Lopez to Taos, where he finds himself in a world of intrigue, caught between feuding ranchers and old legal grievances while searching for a murderer"-- Provided by publisher.
Identifiers: LCCN 2023039930 | ISBN 9781632935489 (paperback) | ISBN 9781611397208 (epub)
Subjects: LCSH: Lopez, Fernando (Fictitious character) | Murder--Investigation--New Mexico--Taos--Fiction. | Taos (N.M.)--Fiction. | LCGFT: Detective and mystery fiction.
Classification: LCC PS3623.I58485 T365 2023 | DDC 813.6--dc23/eng/20230905
LC record available at https://lccn.loc.gov/2023039930

WWW.SUNSTONEPRESS.COM
SUNSTONE PRESS / POST OFFICE BOX 2321 / SANTA FE, NM 87504-2321 /USA
(505) 988-4418

Preface

Taos Vendetta is the third volume of what I call my Taos Trilogy of mysteries. I set the first Taos mystery, *Taos Gothic*, at the magical Mabel Dodge Luhan House in Taos. *Taos Gothic* involves the kidnapping of a Santa Fe historian staying at the Luhan House while researching Willa Cather's stay there in the summer of 1925. *Taos Gothic* is available in a new, revised edition from Sunstone Press.

The second Taos mystery, *Painted Skull Ranch*, I set at a mysterious guest ranch east of Taos modeled on the historic Martinez Hacienda in Taos. *Painted Skull Ranch* involves the sale of illegal drugs and a conspiracy that results in the murder of a nationally known country musician from Austin, Texas.

In all three of these mysteries my former police detective, now private investigator Fernando Lopez, teams up with Taos County Sheriff Hank Mathews. Old friends, the two are well matched: gruff, prickly, and sometimes ornery. Fernando and Hank are not Butch and Sundance pretty boys, just tough, dedicated lawmen who get the job done, whatever it takes.

So here, then, are Fernando and Hank in the final volume of my Taos Trilogy, *Taos Vendetta.*

Off Script

Anne Lewis finished her second margarita and stood up to leave the Cantina at the Sagebrush Inn. Her friend Cassie tried to convince her to stay, but she was tired from a full day of shooting. The cast and crew had waited all day in the Taos Historic Cemetery for the light to be just right, thanks to their impossible to please director, José Sousa. Shooting hadn't started until dusk. By then everyone, including the two leads, were frustrated and prickly. They finished shooting about ten o'clock and rode the vans back to the Sagebrush. She and Cassie and most of the others stopped at the Sagebrush Cantina, an old fashioned saloon with exposed vigas on the ceiling, heavy Mexican furniture, and fireplaces along the walls. Two drinks later she decided to call it quits, dog tired and feeling a bit woozy.

"Aw, come on, have another drink," Cassie said, a tiny blonde with short-cropped hair and tattoos on both arms who worked as one of the make-up artists on the set. "We just got here."

"Nah, I'm beat," Anne said. "After last night with Cowboy Jack, I need to get some sleep."

Cassie laughed, sort of. Cassie didn't approve of her trysts with 'rough trade,' as Cassie referred to the locals. Last night was rough, all right. What Anne could remember!

Out of the corner of her eye Anne spied Cowboy Jack sitting with his friend, who looked even younger than he did. He stared at her from across the room with his white western hat cocked back on his clean-shaven face. No doubt he wanted to hook up with her again tonight. She ignored him, not wishing to have to explain to a twenty-something that some nights she wanted sex, other nights she didn't. And tonight she didn't. End of discussion.

Anne started down the dark hallway to her room rehashing the day's events. She'd waited all day in the midsummer heat for sixty seconds of screen time. She had a small part in the film, another takeoff on the walking dead crap, this one called "The Awakened Dead." The idea was that the dead for some unexplained, ridiculous reason started rising up out of their graves and walking around the streets of Taos. Only a secret chant known by a Pueblo Medicine Man and an herb from Taos Pueblo's Blue Mountain could get them back in the ground. Still, she knew how lucky she was to get the role, given her age. Not to mention the sexual harassment lawsuit she and two other actresses had filed against the executive producer, a Harvey Weinstein type who couldn't keep his hands to himself. She had let the pig maul her once, but never again.

To make the day worse Ted Fisher, the dreaded executive producer, had shown up in Taos this afternoon. In fact, he'd walked into her trailer after they'd quit for the day. Walked right in while she was changing clothes and removing the gross black make-up all the victims of the risen dead had to wear on their faces. She told him to get the hell out, but he started begging her to drop the lawsuit, saying it would ruin his reputation. Boo-hoo! Meanwhile, his electric hands kept touching her in private places she didn't want touched. Finally she pulled away and shoved the old bastard toward the open door. He stumbled out of the trailer with a yelp. Then she slammed the door closed and locked him out. Hopefully that would be her last encounter with the Hollywood pervert while they were shooting. His fat, ugly face and thinning gray hair made her feel sick to her stomach.

On the van driving back to the Sagebrush Anne told Jacqueline, their lead actress, that Ted had accosted her in her trailer earlier that day. Snarky Jacqueline just shrugged and said, "Not my problem." Their relationship had been toxic since their first film, where they competed for the same lead role. Jacqueline won, of course. Jacqueline always won. It was a truism that blond bimbos owned the casting couch.

Fortunately her room at the Sagebrush was on the ground floor. Still unfamiliar with the poorly lit hallway, Anne found what she thought was her room. When the keycard didn't work, she realized her room was the next one down. Once inside, she kicked off her shoes and turned on the lights. She stood in the center of the room facing the patio doors that opened on the swimming pool. Time to decide what to do next. She'd eaten only snacks from the food buffet all afternoon. Should she call room service and order something to eat or just go to bed? Or maybe go for a relaxing swim first and then go to bed? She decided to swim.

So she changed into a bikini and tied her red hair in a tight bun on top of her head. She left her purse in the room, opening the patio door and stepping out into the dark night. The only illumination came from a light in the hallway to the main building. Shadows shrouded the pool, but she could hear the dull hum of its pump. Totally deserted at this time of night. Perfect. She left the door to her room unlocked and closed it behind her.

Anne grabbed a towel from a nearby rack and walked across the pool deck to a chaise near the shallow end. Someone had left a Styrofoam raft on the chaise. She took the raft and left the towel behind, carrying the raft to the steps and down into the cool water. She swam a couple of laps first and then came back for the raft, which danced and bobbed against a skimmer in the shallow end of the pool. She towed the raft back to the steps. Placing the raft between her legs, she then laid back slowly on the Styrofoam and pushed off.

Floating, she began to relax from the stress of the long day. Overhead in the moonless sky she saw a sprinkling of stars, blinking at her through the high clouds. She let herself go, floating every which way the pool jets took her. Every muscle in her body went limp, her mind blank. There was only the sensation of the cool water tickling her flesh, the sweet smell of the Alpine air, the dull hum of the pool pump. She'd never been this relaxed. Ever.

Suddenly she thought she heard a noise in the pool behind her. Not exactly a splash. More of a plop, like a small animal entering the water. Or was it only her imagination?

She listened for a moment but heard nothing. So she let herself go, closing her eyes and letting her arms dangle over the sides of the raft into the water. Limp.

Then she heard the sound again. Definitely a splash. She opened her eyes wide. Just then an arm exploded out of the water. She started to scream. Too late.

The arm grabbed her around the neck from behind and pulled her down into the dark water.

1

Since retiring from the Santa Fe Police Department and hanging his shingle as a private investigator, former Santa Fe police detective Fernando Lopez took his sweet time. He slept late, drank an extra cup of coffee with breakfast, and drove down to his office on Canyon Road whenever he felt like it, usually between nine and ten in the morning every day of the week. The routine provided a structure to his days, which he liked because it kept him busy and not brooding over past mistakes and regrets. At his age he found that if he didn't stay busy he would inevitably gravitate to the dark place. As sure as night follows day.

His wife Estelle approved of his daily routine because it got him out of the house and gave her some free time. Unlike Fernando, Estelle had a naturally cheerful disposition and had no patience for his "moods," as she called them. And unlike Fernando, who had recently retired, Estelle worked long hours for the Saint Francis Immigrant Outreach Program, a church-sponsored nonprofit that provided food and clothing and other services to Santa Fe's growing immigrant community. In fact, her workload kept increasing as more and more immigrants came through Santa Fe, a sanctuary city.

Fernando hated to admit it, but he and Estelle were no longer as close as they once were. Estelle had grown more religious over the years, working for the outreach program and attending mass almost every Sunday. He had grown in the opposite direction. After thirty years of police work he'd lost his faith. He believed in a material world, pure and simple. He still went to church with Estelle on Christmas Eve and Easter Sunday just to appease her, but that was as far as he was willing to go. So he found it better for both of them--and their marriage--if he spent a good part of every day at his office, a former garage that his old friend Ruby Montez had allowed him to remodel and use rent-free.

Ruby, a potter by trade and a former City Council member, owned the gallery next door. She'd inherited the gallery from her dead ex-husband Jimmy Mackey and recently renamed it the Three Cities of

Spain, after a popular Canyon Road restaurant that closed years ago. Ruby also owned a pottery co-op in the Railyard District where she allowed other female potters to work free of charge.

This morning Fernando left his house on Acequia Madre Street later than usual. By the time he pulled into the parking lot between Ruby's gallery and Essentia, a local sex shop, the clock on the dash of his Jeep Cherokee read nearly ten thirty. He parked in the back of the lot, near his Private Eye sign. He climbed out of his Cherokee and walked down the gravel path to his office. He could hear Ruby laughing inside her gallery as he opened his door and changed the window sign from Closed to Open. He raised the bank of windows that looked over Alameda Street below to get some fresh air. The small office still smelled of new carpet and wood paneling. Given the size of the room, he'd kept his furniture to a minimum: a desk, a bookcase, a couple of chairs, and his latest purchase, a mini refrigerator where he kept bottles of water for the morning and Modelo for the afternoon.

Since it was barely ten thirty, he grabbed a bottle of water from the refrigerator and sat at his desk. The message light on his desk phone blinked wildly at him. Two new messages. He expected another crank call. Every other day he received a crazy message from a jokester, either aliens had landed in Fort Marcy Park or the governor was posing nude on the Santa Fe Plaza. Today, though, when he pushed the button he heard a familiar voice: "Fernando, are you available to give me a hand today? I'd be mighty grateful."

Fernando recognized the voice of Taos County Sheriff Hank Mathews. He'd worked with Hank on a couple of recent homicide cases up in Taos. A good man. The second message, also from Hank, sounded more desperate: "Fernando, I could really use your help. I got a dead movie actress in the swimming pool at the Sagebrush Inn. Looks like she was murdered. To make matters worse, I got a whole movie crew mad as hell at me. Could you help out with this? We're short-handed big time. I'd appreciate it, old buddy."

Fernando hit the redial button. Moments later Hank answered: "Fernando! Damn, I been trying to get you all morning. Could you come up and lend a hand with this homicide at the Sagebrush? I got two deputies on medical leave after a shoot-out responding to a domestic violence report in Dixon. Then this feud between the Jack Ryan and Eloy Lucero clans has flared up again. Nobody wants anything to do with those crazy bastards. We're so short I don't know what the hell to do. I'll tell you what--I could swear you in so's we could put you on the payroll. Just until I can round up more deputies."

"No, that's not necessary," Fernando said. "I owe you twice over.

You saved the day at the Mabel Dodge Luhan House and again at Painted Skull Ranch. Both of my last cases up there."

"Well, suit yourself," Hank said.

Fernando checked the time. "Where are you now?"

"I'm still at the Sagebrush," Hank said. "Forensics just left with the body. Not a pretty sight after being in the swimming pool all night."

"Did she drown?" Fernando asked.

Hank chuckled. "Yeah, with a little help from someone. One of the groundskeepers found the body this morning. Forensics thinks she'd been in the pool all night. I'm looking for people who were with her last night. Which ain't easy because there's a whole lotta people in the movie crew to interview."

"Okay, Hank. I'm on my way."

Fernando decided not to tell Estelle about Taos. She would be working for the outreach program all day anyway. Lately she hadn't been getting home until after seven o'clock. Hopefully he would be back in Santa Fe well before that.

He erased his messages on the machine and put his Closed sign back in the window as he left. He drove his Cherokee down Canyon Road to the Paseo and followed it around to the entrance to Highway 285 North, where he stopped for gas. Then he commenced the all-too-familiar journey, passing Tesuque, the Santa Fe Opera, and Nambé. In Española he stopped at his favorite Whataburger for a quick Green Chile Cheeseburger and then continued north on Highway 68, known as the Low Road to Taos. The highway followed the Rio Grande River as it snaked its way up the canyon to Taos, with the river on the left and red sandstone cliffs on the right. The dusty green mesas on either side of the canyon were dotted with juniper and piñon trees.

Nearing Pilar Fernando saw whitewater rafts and kayaks bouncing through the rapids, heading downriver. In a parking area up ahead a gathering of commercial trucks with trailers unloaded more rafts and kayaks while their customers waited in line, all wearing orange lifejackets. Fernando slowed down to gawk at the boaters. Then he sped up through the winding canyons that led to the Rio Grande Gorge Visitor Center. Finally he climbed the long hill up to Ranchos de Taos, with the famous church painted and photographed by a zillion artists.

Once through Ranchos de Taos the highway ran straight ahead to the 13,000-foot Taos Mountains. Fernando ignored the fast food restaurants and strip malls along either side of the road. Tourist vans, SUVs, and buses clogged the highway leading into town. Midsummer madness. Fortunately, the turn-off to the Sagebrush was only a few blocks down on the left.

Turning into the entrance to the Sagebrush he saw a fleet of trailers and RVs parked off to the side of the parking lot. That would be the movie company, all their cameras and equipment packed up and portable. A group of a dozen or so people stood around the vehicles waiting. None of them looked very happy by the way they gestured at one another.

Fernando drove around front and pulled into a parking space near the front entrance to the 100-year-old adobe building, with vigas protruding from the brown stucco and heavy wooden doors and window frames. He set the brake and climbed out of his Cherokee, noticing Hank's cruiser parked on the far side of the hotel all by its lonesome. Old Hank must be short-handed, if he came by himself. He stepped into the spacious lobby that always made him feel like stepping back in time. The interior of the hotel was classic Taos: thick adobe walls with a rough coating of stucco, exposed vigas on the ceiling, and various Southwestern antiques hanging on the walls, along with stuffed animal heads and paintings of famous Native Americans and Taoseños. Resembled a damn Wild West museum.

Fernando noticed a gathering of Sagebrush employees behind the front counter. Otherwise the lobby looked empty. An older man wearing a tan suit without a tie came over to greet him. "Hello, I'm sorry to have to tell you that we're closed temporarily," he said, a tall thin man with white hair and a red, ruddy face. "We hope to open later this afternoon."

Fernando nodded and gave the man his card. "I'm looking for Sheriff Hank Mathews. He's asked me to help with his investigation."

The man in the suit introduced himself as Gary Clark, general manager of the Sagebrush. "Please. Follow me. I believe he's in the room occupied by Miss Lewis, the young woman who drowned."

Fernando noticed Clark's choice of words: drowned rather than murdered. He followed Clark down a long dark hallway to a room near the end. The door to the room remained wide open. He could hear Hank's voice inside.

Clark stopped Fernando before he could enter the room. "We have to get this under control, you know," the manager whispered. "This is very bad for business. Very bad."

"Of course," Fernando said, and stepped into the room. He closed the door behind him.

Hank stood in the center of the room talking to a young woman with short blond hair sitting on a king-size bed. The woman held a box of tissues in her hand. The tissues and her red eyes indicated she had been crying for some time.

Hank waved, a big man wearing a black Stetson and a Colt .45 on his hip. "This here's former detective Fernando Lopez--he's helping me with the investigation," he explained to the woman.

She nodded and dried her eyes.

"Fernando, this is Cassie Jenkins, she was with the woman who drowned last night. They were good friends."

Fernando nodded. "Sorry for your loss."

The petite blonde lowered her head. She took a deep breath and raised her head again. "Like I said, we came back to the Sagebrush about ten thirty or eleven. Most everyone stopped at the Cantina for a drink. It had been a long day because we had to wait for just the right lighting. Anne had two margaritas and then decided to call it a night. She said she was tired and needed to sleep. That was the last time I saw her, walking out of the Cantina."

"She didn't try to contact you after she left the bar? Call you from her room?" Hank asked.

"No," Cassie said, sniffing.

Fernando grabbed a nearby chair and moved it closer to the bed. "So, Cassie, who might want to harm Anne? Did she have any enemies? People she had quarreled with? People who might want to harm her?"

Cassie paused, wiping her eyes with a tissue. "Well...do you know about her lawsuit against Ted Fisher?"

Fernando shook his head. "No, why don't you tell us? And who's this Ted Fisher?"

"He's the executive producer of the movie we're filming here," Cassie said. "He's kind of a Harvey Weinstein type, you know? Can't keep his hands off women, especially young actresses. Anne and two other women from L.A. have accused him of sexual assault. One of the other women claims he raped her at the Beverly Hills Hotel. Whenever Ted came around, Anne would leave. She refused to talk to him. He scared her."

"Did this Ted character ever make advances to you?" Hank asked, joining the conversation.

"No, I just do make-up, I'm not an actress," Cassie said. "He only goes after young actresses. As far as I know."

Fernando raised his hand to ask another question, but Cassie cut him off before he could speak.

"The really weird thing, though," she said, glancing from Fernando to Hank, "Was that Ted showed up on the set yesterday. He never does that. I mean, executive producers handle money, they stay away from the set during shooting. So it was weird to see him yesterday."

"Did Anne say anything about Ted appearing?" Fernando asked.

"Yeah, actually she did. She said she threw him out of her trailer. She didn't give me any details, but I imagine he was trying to talk her out of continuing with the lawsuit. That's all I know."

Fernando nodded. "Anybody else you can think of that Anne had quarreled with?"

"Sure, Anne didn't get along with Jacqueline Bonet, the lead actress in the movie," Cassie said. "They fought all the time. They had a long history of competing for the same roles, but Jacqueline almost always got the part. Most of Anne's roles were minor. Like her role in this movie."

"The Awakened Dead?" Hank drawled.

Cassie nodded.

"So did Anne and Jacqueline's disagreements ever get physical?" Fernando asked.

"No, they just screamed at each other. Stuff like that."

"Anybody else you can think of?"

"Not exactly," she said, pausing for a moment as if deciding whether to continue. "There's a guy she called Cowboy Jack. His name was Jack Jr. I can't remember his last name. He comes to the bar nearly every night looking for action. On a couple of nights Anne hooked up with him."

"By hooked up, you mean had sex," Hank interjected.

Cassie nodded. "I told her to stay away from him. That he was a roughneck and couldn't be trusted. But she slept with him anyway. Anne was a headstrong woman. When she was horny, she was horny! Anyway, after that night he started showing up every evening. Finally she had sex with him again two nights ago. That's why she was so tired last night."

"Was this Jack Jr. in the bar last night?" Hank asked.

She nodded. "Just sitting there watching Anne."

"What's this guy look like?" Hank asked.

"Young, nice looking, early twenties," Cassie said. "He wears a western hat, kinda like yours, except it's white."

Hank looked at Fernando and nodded. "Okay. How long will you be in town in case we have any more questions?"

"We're supposed to be done shooting here by the end of the week, but I don't know. The director's so fussy we might be here forever."

Hank handed her one of his cards. "Give me a call if you think of anything else. Anything at all."

Fernando did likewise, handing her a card.

Cassie took her box of tissues and walked out of the room. Hank replaced her on the bed, bouncing up and down. "What do you think?"

Fernando shrugged. "What did Forensics find when they went through the room earlier?"

"Couple of used condoms in the bathroom trash," Hank said. "Not much else. They took fingerprint and DNA samples, so we'll know more when the results come in. Maybe tomorrow."

Fernando stood and looked out the open patio door at the swimming pool. Sawhorses and yellow caution tape closed off the pool. He eased out the door and walked across the deck to the shallow end of the pool.

Hank followed.

"Where did you find her?" Fernando asked, looking down at the steps leading into the water.

Hank pointed to the right side of the pool. "Next to the skimmer in the shallow end. Her bikini top was over in the deep end. Someone must have ripped it off before or after killing her."

"Why? Was she attacked sexually?" Fernando asked. "Is there any indication of sexual penetration?"

Hank shook his head. "Forensics doesn't think so."

"Then maybe the top came lose during the struggle," Fernando said.

Hank didn't respond.

Fernando stared at the skimmer.

"Here, have a look," Hank said, pulling his cell phone out of a back pocket. "I took this photo for reference."

Fernando glanced at the photo--a bloated, wrinkled white body of a half-naked woman partially submerged near the skimmer, her face surrounded by a halo of fiery red hair flayed in the water. Her mouth and eyes remained wide open, frozen in her final horrified seconds.

"Yeah, quite a sight," Fernando said finally and turned away.

"Notice the bruising around her neck," Hank said. "Forensics thinks someone held her under water, maybe from behind."

"Why from behind?"

"Because there aren't any finger indentations on the neck," Hank said but didn't explain.

Just then they heard footsteps approaching on the deck behind them. Hank spun around, hand on his holster.

"Sorry, didn't mean to scare you," the stranger said, holding up his hands. He looked around fifty years old, chubby with a pock-marked face. Dressed in slacks and a white shirt, his black hair was long and slicked back. Greasy.

Hank laughed. "You don't scare me, friend. What can I do for you?"

"Ted Fisher," the man said and held out his hand, which Hank ignored. "I'm the executive producer of the movie we're shooting. We have a shoot scheduled in just over an hour. Everyone's outside by the trailers now waiting for the okay to leave. We're already behind schedule and over-budget, so I hope you understand that we need to get going. We can't wait around here all day while you guys conduct your investigation. None of us had anything to do with Anne's drowning."

Hank raised his hand. "So you want permission to leave, is that what you're saying?"

"Yes, because we have a schedule to meet and my people need to work to get paid!" Fisher said emphatically. "I mean, I'm sorry about Anne. It was a terrible thing to have happened, but you need to find out who murdered her and let us get back to work, okay?"

Hank gave the fancy man the Evil Eye. He pushed back the Stetson on his head and said in his best drawl, "That right? Well here's the thing, fella. We need to question both you and Jacqueline Bonet first and probably a whole lotta other people later. We can do it now, or we can do it later at wherever you're shooting."

A shadow of a frown came across Fisher's face. He looked worried. "Why do you want to question me? I wasn't even here last night. I'm staying at the Taos Inn back in town."

"Because Anne Lewis and two other women are suing you for sexual assault," Hank said bluntly.

Fisher backed up. "That's just a terrible misunderstanding. The lawsuit has no merit."

Hank ignored Fisher's protestations. "So where are you shooting today?"

"We're shooting in the historical cemetery again today. You can find us there or in our trailers," Fisher said.

"Oh, we'll find you," Hank said. "You can count on that."

2

By the time they finished at the Sagebrush and drove to Kit Carson Park it was past three o'clock. Fernando rode with Hank to expedite matters. The movie trailers were parked on the south side of the parking lot, which bordered the Taos Historical Cemetery. Hank pulled in behind the last trailer, killed the cruiser's big engine, and set the brake. "Let's do this," Hank said.

Fernando followed Hank around the line of trailers to the edge of the cemetery. From there they looked out on an improbable scene. A dozen or so extras stood behind graves waiting for the shooting to begin. All wore tattered black clothes, rags really, with faces discolored and distorted by thick black make-up. They looked like a bunch of kids gathered for a Halloween event, except the kids here were grown-ups and the event was a multi-million dollar movie. Toward the front of the cemetery a dolly track had been laid with the camera in place, ready to follow the action. The camera crew and the boom operator stood at attention, waiting for the action to start. Just outside the cemetery gate stood a group of men and women wearing headphones and carrying clipboards. One especially tall man in the center wearing a leather vest and sunglasses stood talking to a young woman who listened intently to his every word. He was clearly the director giving her directions for the next scene.

Fernando thought he recognized the woman. Even though she was made up to look like a country lass, wearing a flowery cotton dress and carrying a bouquet of flowers, he recognized her face. "That's Cassie Jenkins," he said to Hank, who was also staring at her. "She told me she was a make-up artist, not an actress."

They waited until the director finished his instructions to Cassie. When he left to talk to the camera crew, they hurried over to Cassie before she disappeared. She seemed surprised to see them.

"Cassie, I see you're gonna be in the movie," Hank said. "We didn't know you were an actress?"

She blushed. "Well, José asked me to fill in for Anne. It's a small role, but who knows, maybe this will be my big break," she said, beaming.

"Maybe so," Hank said.

Fernando stepped up. "Where's Jacqueline? She's still the lead, right?"

Cassie nodded. "Hers is the second trailer," she said pointing to the line of trailers in the parking lot. Then she excused herself and disappeared.

"Her big break? That's damn convenient for her, isn't it," Hank said as they walked to the trailers.

"Maybe too convenient," Fernando said.

They walked by the open door of the first trailer, filled with video screens and banks of electronic equipment. The door of the second trailer was closed with a 'Do Not Disturb' sign front and center.

Hank knocked on the door anyway.

"Go away!" came a shrill voice.

Hank opened the door and stepped inside. "Howdy, ma'am."

"What do you think you're doing? Get out of here!" Jacqueline ordered.

Fernando saw immediately why she would get all the roles over Anne Lewis. Jacqueline was drop-dead gorgeous: a perfect body, strawberry blond hair and a complexion that glowed. All sexed up waiting for her shoot, she wore a tight mini skirt and an even tighter sleeveless blouse that revealed all the right curves. She stood in front of her dressing table glaring at them.

"Hank Mathews, Taos County Sheriff," Hank introduced himself. "We aim to talk to you about the drowning of Anne Lewis. Now if you want, I can have you brought to the station for questioning. Or we can talk here, right now. Up to you."

Jacqueline changed her tone of voice. Not what you'd call friendly, but at least not hostile. "I'm sorry, but I don't know anything about her drowning. Why would I?"

"Did you see her last night, after you returned to the Sagebrush?" Hank asked. "You all stopped in the Cantina for drinks, right? Were you with her?"

She shook her head. "No, I went back to my room immediately. Unlike Anne, I have a major role in the movie, so I had to prepare my lines for today. I had to work."

"Plus," Fernando interjected, "you and Anne weren't on friendly terms. In fact, you disliked each other, right?"

Jacqueline turned to Fernando. "I wanted nothing to do with Anne. She was a slut. She was always sleeping with 'rough trade,' low-class louts she met at the bars. Lots of her friends warned her to be careful, but she would never listen to anyone. Given her reputation, it was a miracle she could get even minor roles."

Fernando nodded. "You think that's what happened last night? That a person she picked up at the Cantina killed her?"

"I wouldn't be surprised."

"Do you remember seeing her with a man wearing a western hat?" Fernando asked. "A young man she called Cowboy Jack?"

"In the Cantina? No, I told you I wasn't in the Cantina last night. I rarely go into bars I'm not familiar with. And never with locals."

Hank changed the topic. "What about this lawsuit Anne Lewis and some other women have filed against your executive producer, Ted Fisher?"

"Ted? I did see him at the Sagebrush. He was with José when we unloaded the van."

"Well, now that's interesting," Hank said. "He told us he was staying at the Taos Inn."

Jacqueline shook her head. "I don't know where he's staying, but he was at the Sagebrush after last night's shoot."

"And what about the lawsuit?"

"Don't know," she said. "Ted's never harassed me, ever. And I've known him for going on ten years. But you know what, it wouldn't surprise me if Anne and the others initiated the harassment. It was common knowledge that Anne tried to sleep her way to the top. To be blunt."

Fernando laughed. "You really disliked her, didn't you? Why was that? Were you somehow intimidated by her?"

She looked horrified. "Oh, don't play drugstore psychiatrist with me. I don't have time for this. I have a shoot in less than an hour. I need to go over my lines. So please, get out."

Hank tipped his Stetson. "We'll be in touch."

Fernando followed Hank outside. They walked across the parking lot to the fence surrounding the western side of the cemetery. From there they had a clear view of the shoot about to unfold. Cassie stood just outside the cemetery gate holding a bouquet of flowers. The extras, covered in black rags and make-up, waited behind the larger gravestones. The cameraman and boom operator were set up on a dolly waiting to follow Cassie into the graveyard on a track erected on the grass parallel to the sidewalk.

When José, the director, gave the signal and the clapperboard sounded, Cassie came walking spritely through the gate of the cemetery. She looked cheerful and ebullient in her loose cotton dress with a bright blue ribbon in her blond hair. She raised her bouquet of flowers and sniffed their sweet fragrance and then skipped happily down the path, not aware of the dark shadows that awaited her. The dark ones lurked behind the ancient weathered tombstones. They began to awaken from their frozen postures, seemingly rising from their graves. Their bony hands reached out toward the tiny blond woman as she grew closer.

The dolly followed Cassie as she skipped unaware into the heart of darkness. Suddenly the dark figures jumped out from behind the tombstones and pounced on the unsuspecting Cassie. She screamed as they tore at her clothing and scattered her flowers. Intentionally, of course, her milky white breasts spilled out of her dress to titillate the cameras--and the intended audience. Growling and fighting with each other like a pack of wild dogs, the black bodies piled on the screaming woman. After a few seconds the screaming stopped. Cassie's character lay dead. The mass of black bodies began to untangle. They arose one by one, their faces covered with fake blood dripping from their open mouths.

"Cut!" the director shouted.

The action stopped.

The extras walked nonchalantly back to the cemetery gate as though they were out for a Sunday stroll. Cassie, on the other hand, struggled to get up from the muck, her cotton dress now shredded and covered with red and black goop. Even so, she laughed and shook off the goop as best she could. Then she joined the others at the gate. All the actors huddled around the director.

Fernando laughed at Hank's reaction to what they had just witnessed. The big man shook his head and pawed the ground with his boot.

"What horseshit!" Hank said finally. "Do people actually watch this stuff?"

"Don't ask me," Fernando said.

"Let's get the hell out of here."

Hank led the way back to the cruiser. He opened the door but paused a moment and leaned on the roof of the car. "Two down. Now we need to find Ted Fisher. If he was at the Sagebrush last night, I wanna know what the hell he was doing there."

"And don't forget Cowboy Jack," Fernando added.

"Yeah, Cowboy Jack," Hank said. "If it's who I think it is, I'd sure enough like to forget him."

"Yeah? Why's that?" Fernando asked.

"Well, the only Jack Junior I know around these parts is Jack Ryan Junior," Hank said. "I told you about the feud between the Jack Ryan and

Eloy Lucero clans out near Questa, both of whom I've known forever. Old Jack accused Eloy of grazing livestock illegally on BLM land Jack leased from the government. So Jack decided to take matters into his own hands and shot some of Eloy's animals. Then Old Eloy accused Jack of the same thing and decided to take matters into his own hands and shot Jack dead. Since then all hell's broken loose on the mountain. Jack's oldest son, Morris, shot and killed Eloy, after which Eloy's oldest son, Armando, shot and killed Morris. Now Jack's second son, Cowboy Jack, has vowed to kill Armando. Since then they've been trying to pick each other off one at a time. I'm telling you, every last one of the idiots should be in jail."

Fernando shook his head, trying to keep the names straight. The last thing he wanted was to get involved in a violent family feud.

"That's why," Hank added.

"Well, hell, let's forget about Cowboy Jack for now and question Ted Fisher first," Fernando said. "He told us he's staying at the Taos Inn, so why don't we pay him a visit. It's getting late, he might be back at the hotel."

Hank smiled. "First sensible thing I've heard all day. Maybe we can invite him for drinks. He seemed like a sociable type."

"I'm sure. Especially with the women."

Hank laughed and climbed into the cruiser. Since the Taos Inn was only a couple of blocks away, he drove to the nearest side street and parked there. Then the two of them walked to the Paseo and around to the front entrance of the Taos Inn. Like most buildings in downtown Taos, the Taos Inn included several wings spliced together over the years. The main building on the Paseo dated from the 1930s, but some of the adobe wings in back dated from the 1880s.

They walked into the lobby, a tall-ceiling building with a second floor balcony visible along one wall where several guest rooms looked down on the lobby. The first thing you saw when you stepped inside was a small fountain in the center of the room bordered by four enormous log pillars holding up a ceiling built of latillas in quadrants. The tips of the quadrants met at a round skylight in the center of the ceiling. Everything else about the lobby was equally eccentric, with rounded door passages leading into the interior of the inn and hand-carved wooden signs and furniture. On the front desk a hand-carved phoenix, the bird of resurrection, greeted every guest who entered the front doors of the venerable Taos Inn.

Fernando held back and let Hank approach the front counter, where a young man in a white shirt and bolo tie greeted him

"Howdy," Hank said, and showed the young man his credentials.

"We're here to see Ted Fisher. Could you ring his room?"

"Sure," the clerk said. He picked up the phone and buzzed Fisher's room and waited. "Sorry, he doesn't answer. Do you want to leave a message?"

"No sir. We'll wait," Hank said.

Fernando took a seat on a bench in the corner of the lobby. Hank paced back and forth in the lobby a few times and then checked his watch. Finally he joined Fernando on the bench.

They waited almost an hour before Ted Fisher walked into the lobby wearing a camera vest with what looked like a Leica and several lenses in the various pockets of the vest. Heading for the front desk, Fisher spotted them on the bench and stopped dead in his tracks. He turned and slowly ambled over to where they were sitting. From the expression on his face it was obvious that he was not happy to see them.

"Gentlemen," Fisher said and pulled up a chair. "I thought we finished our business back at the Sagebrush. What can I do for you now?"

"No such luck," Hank said sadly, shaking his head. "Turns out you lied to us. We have a witness who saw you at the Sagebrush last night, just before Anne Lewis was murdered. You wanna tell us what you were doing there? And no more lies."

Fisher glanced around the lobby, as though he felt trapped. "Okay. I was there briefly. No more than fifteen or twenty minutes. I didn't think it was worth mentioning to you this morning."

"Why not? That would be just enough time to kill Anne Lewis," Fernando said.

"No!" Fisher shot back. "I didn't kill Anne."

"Then what were you doing at the Sagebrush?" Hank asked. "Since you're staying here, at the Taos Inn."

Fisher looked down at his hands, a pained expression on his chubby face. He sighed. "I went there to see Anne--to try to persuade her to drop her lawsuit. But she wasn't in her room. I went back twice and knocked on the door but she never answered. So I left about eleven thirty, maybe a little earlier. That's the truth. I tried, but I never saw her."

"Wait a minute," Fernando interrupted. "You said you were only there fifteen or twenty minutes. Now you're saying you went to her door three times. What else are you lying about?"

Fisher had started to sweat now. They could see the sweat beading on his forehead.

"Okay, maybe I was there for half an hour, but no more than that."

"Do you have a witness who'll verify that?" Fernando asked.

"No. How could I, I was alone," Fisher said.

Hank gave Fisher the Evil Eye. "Un-huh. Well, sir, here's the problem. Forensics found two used condoms in Anne Lewis' room. We need a DNA sample from you to verify your claims. If what you say is true, then you surely won't mind stopping by my office tomorrow morning to give us your fingerprints and a DNA sample."

"What? Are you saying I'm a suspect, because if you are...." Fisher said, starting to get angry.

"Listen to me!" Hank boomed. "What I'm saying is this. Either you come to the office and give me the sample, or I will arrest you on suspicion of murder and force you to take a DNA test. New Mexico and Federal law allow me to do just that. Do you understand?"

Fisher shook his head, muttering to himself. He glanced from Hank to Fernando. "Should I bring a lawyer?"

Hank opened his arms. "That's up to you. If your DNA isn't on those condoms or in Anne Lewis' room, you probably don't need a lawyer. If it is, then I suggest you get yourself lawyered up real fast with a lawyer who knows criminal law, New Mexico style."

Fisher turned to Fernando as though looking for help. None came.

"And I mean a damned good lawyer," Hank said and handed Fisher a business card.

3

Fernando awoke in an unfamiliar bed in an unfamiliar room. It took him a few moments to remember where he was and how he got there. Yesterday evening, after dinner with Hank at Michael's Kitchen, he decided it was too late to drive back to Santa Fe. Instead, he decided to stay in Taos so they could get an early start and continue their investigation today. In Taos he usually stayed at the El Pueblo Lodge, near Michael's Kitchen, but this time he took a room at the Sagebrush Inn in order to keep an eye on their chief suspects and the rest of the movie crowd. His courtyard room lay directly across the courtyard and pool from the room Anne Lewis had occupied before her murder.

He gathered his wits for a few moments and then climbed out of bed and splashed water on his face. Then he brewed himself a cup of coffee with the automatic coffeemaker in his room and sat down to review his notes. Of the three suspects they'd interviewed yesterday, Ted Fisher seemed the most likely candidate. Engaged in bitter litigation with Anne and two other women, he had admitted visiting her twice on the day she was murdered, once at her trailer, which resulted in a violent confrontation, and once unsuccessfully outside the door of her room. Jacqueline Bonet and Cassie Jenkins were also possibilities, Jacqueline because she disliked Anne and disapproved of Anne's reckless behavior, and Cassie because of professional jealousy. What was it Cassie had said? That Anne's death could be her big break in the movies.

That left Cowboy Jack, yet to be interviewed. He was their unknown, their possible number four. The odd man out.

Their plan today was to visit Cowboy Jack at the Ryan family's ranch near Questa. Cowboy Jack had wild sex with Anne the night before she died and apparently showed up at the Sagebrush wanting more good times on the very night she was murdered. Just what all he was willing to do to bring about those good times was the question now.

After he cleaned up, Fernando walked across the courtyard to the Sagebrush Grill for breakfast. The Grill had exposed vigas on the ceiling, dark clunky tables and chairs, and an adobe partial wall for some reason painted midnight blue. He sat at a corner table where he could observe the other customers but saw no one he recognized from the movie crowd. When the server appeared, a flustered young woman with a nervous smile and a long braid down her back, he ordered his usual breakfast of Huevos Rancheros. He ate quickly, so he could meet Hank at the appointed hour.

Even so, he was a half-hour late by the time he drove over to the Taos County Sheriff's Office on Lovato Place. He parked the Cherokee behind the nondescript one-story building and hurried into the office. He found Hank pacing back and forth in his office, waiting. Hank was not a patient man.

"Howdy there, Sleeping Beauty. You just missed Ted Fisher. He stopped by and gave us a DNA sample, sans lawyer. I guess he thinks he's not in danger."

"Which means he's probably not," Fernando said. "If that was his used condom in Anne's room, he would have brought a lawyer. Or two."

"Yep, I agree," Hank responded. "So you ready to pay Cowboy Jack a surprise visit?"

Fernando laughed. "Ready and willing. Let's see what Cowboy Jack has to say for himself."

Just then Roy, one of Hank's deputies, came limping down the hallway using a cane. A small, thin man with a buzzed head, Roy looked positively emaciated. He'd been wounded in the shootout at Painted Skull Ranch earlier this year.

Fernando was shocked to see Roy's condition. "Hey, Roy. Are you going to be okay?"

Roy grimaced as he walked toward the front office. "Oh, I'm healing...slowly. The bullet entered my thigh and traveled all the way to my hip. Busted up the hip joint. I'm in physical therapy three afternoons a week. Doctors tell me I should be walking without a cane in another month or so. It's been a long road back. I feel as useless as tits on a boar."

Hank turned to Fernando. "Roy comes in mornings to help out in the office. We're mighty short-handed."

"I could come along this morning to provide back up," Roy said.

"Nah, that ain't necessary," Hank said. "You follow the doc's orders. We need you back full-strength as soon as possible."

Roy nodded. "Suit yourself," he said, hobbling back down the hallway.

Hank loaded and buckled on his duty belt and checked his Colt .45. "Let's go see Cowboy Jack."

Fernando followed Hank outside. He stopped at the Cherokee to get his Smith & Wessen .41 Magnum and then climbed into the cruiser's front passenger seat and buckled up. He'd ridden with Hank enough times to know that seatbelts were a definite requirement.

Hank revved the engine and drove off fast, swerving onto Paseo del Pueblo Sur heading north. Not even heavy traffic could slow down Hank. He switched on the siren to force the surprised tourists into the right lane and honked at those drivers slow to move over. They raced out Highway 64 to 522 and headed due north toward Arroyo Hondo, San Cristobal, and Questa, a distance of about thirty miles. Soon the Wild Rivers National Recreation Area appeared on the left and the Sangre de Cristo Mountains on the right. They caught glimpses of the twelve thousand foot peaks as they sped up the highway.

Just past San Cristobal Hank started mumbling about all the work awaiting him back at the office. Paperwork, a summons to serve, an overdue report, and the list went on.

"And you can't find new recruits to replace the deputies you've lost?" Fernando asked.

"Hah! No one wants the job, too dangerous," Hank said. "Hell, half the time we're outgunned when we arrive at a robbery or even a domestic dispute. Everybody and his uncle is armed to the teeth out here in the country. And I'm not talking about pistols. Most of these bastards have assault weapons. Military style!"

Fernando shook his head. "I can imagine. It's no better in the city."

Hank mumbled something and then passed a beat-up Volvo going well below the speed limit.

"So what haven't you told me about Cowboy Jack and this feud between the Ryans and Luceros?" Fernando asked.

"Well, like I said, the feud's been going on for years over who has the lease on that BLM land," Hank said. "I told you how both Jack Ryan and Eloy Lucero were shot dead. Then this summer their sons joined the fun when Armando, the oldest Lucero son, shot and killed Morris, the oldest Ryan son. Gunshots, ambushes, you name it. The neighbors down below the two ranches are complaining. Sam Perkins stopped by the office the other day and said it was like a shooting range up there on the mountain and asked me why the hell I'm not stopping it. I asked him just how in the hell did he expect me to do that, and do you know what he said?"

Fernando shook his head.

Hank laughed. "He said 'shoot the sonsabitches, all of them.'"

"Any arrests so far?"

"Hell, we don't know who to arrest," Hank said. "Everyone claims self-defense, stand your ground, kiss my ass, whatever. Who knows who's shooting first? We don't have any witnesses up there. No live witnesses anyways."

Fernando nodded. "How many Ryans are we talking about?"

"In the clan? Well, they're thinned out some these days, now that Morris was shot and killed. You got Ruth, the mother. She's the matriarch of the clan, tougher than nails. Then there's Cowboy Jack and Donnie, the youngest. Still a teenager, sixteen or thereabouts."

"And the Luceros?" Fernando asked.

"Armando's the one to watch out for there," Hank said. "He's the oldest son. He's the one who gunned down Morris. Then there's the mother, Isabel, and her two other kids: Tony and Rosalia, the youngest."

Hank slowed down as they approached the tiny village of Questa, a collection of small shops and convenience stores. At the Questa Visitor Center he turned off on Cabresto Canyon Road, an unpaved forest road that climbed up to the 13,000-foot Latir Peak in the Sangre de Cristo Mountains. Eventually they came to an unmaintained dirt road off to the left.

Hank turned onto the narrow dirt road. The unwieldy cruiser bounced over the deep ruts and rocks along the road. The road dead-ended at a T. Hank pointed to the left. "The Ryan Ranch is this way, the Lucero Ranch is to the right and further up the mountain."

The dirt drive leading to the Ryan Ranch was just as bad as the road in. Hank had to stop more than once to ease the cruiser over a particularly deep rut or around a buried rock. They stopped once to allow a solitary cow to meander across the road in front of them. The cow stopped in the middle of the road, turned to look at them, and then moved on to the other side.

Up ahead they saw a metal fence and gate across the road. Above the gate hung a metal sign etched with the words: 'Ryan Ranch'. Coming closer, they saw the gate was locked with a heavy chain and padlock. The fence on either side of the gate dipped down into deep ravines, making it impossible to circumvent the gate with the cruiser or any other motorized vehicle.

Hank parked in front of the gate and scrambled out of the cruiser.

"They really roll out the welcome mat here, don't they?" Fernando joked, joining Hank at the gate.

Hank smiled. "Yessir, I'd like to meet the fool who said your typical country folk were friendly."

Fernando pointed to the ravine on the right. "Looks like we can squeeze around the fence down there. Unless you want to try climbing over the gate."

"Hah! No climbing for me. I'm gonna have a hell of a time going down into the arroyo, not to mention getting around that fence, what with my arthritic knees," Hank said. "You go first, I'll follow."

With that, Fernando climbed into the ravine, scraping through a tangle of sage and saltbush. He squeezed through the gap between the fence and the far side of the ravine and then watched Hank swat his way through the underbrush.

By the time Hank made it to the road on the other side of the gate he was cursing and favoring his right knee. "I'm coming, hold your horses," Hank said.

They trudged up the slow rise of the road, Fernando in front and Hank trying to keep up. Overhead the sun scalded the sandy road white. Heat waves rippled their view of the emerging ranch, which included a scattering of buildings around a central square of open ground. Fernando saw an L-shaped ranch house with a long porch in front and a large unpainted barn further back. A maze of corrals and two smaller buildings surrounded the barn. Looked like a pump house and a tool shed.

"What the hell is that?" Hank asked, pointing to what looked like a round bunker about fifty yards away. Between them and the house.

The structure appeared to consist of stacked adobe bricks, the ancient building material of the Southwest made from a mixture of mud and straw and sometimes ash and then dried in the sun. As they approached the structure a deer rifle with scope popped up over the top of the stacked adobes followed by the head of what looked like a teenage boy aiming the rifle directly at them.

"Just hold it right there," the kid said.

Fernando reached for his Smith & Wessen, but Hank grabbed his hand and then turned toward the kid.

"Hold on there, Donnie, it's Hank. You remember me, the sheriff."

Donnie did not respond.

"What the hell are you doing out here, son?" Hank asked. "You could hurt someone pointing a rifle like that."

"I'm watching for the Luceros, that's what I'm doing," Donnie said. "They killed my daddy and my brother. I aim to kill one of them."

Hank raised his hands, pleading with the kid. "You don't want to get involved in this killing nonsense, Donnie. You've got your whole life ahead of you. Don't waste it on something like this."

Again Donnie did not respond.

Hank sighed. "I'm here to speak to your mama."

Finally Donnie lowered his rifle and stood. With fair hair and freckles, the kid looked very young, sixteen at the most. A baby. "She's over at the barn waiting for Jack Junior."

"Much obliged," Hank said as they walked by the adobe bunker.

Fernando noticed a folding chair and even a small tent pitched behind the thick adobe wall. Was the kid camping in the bunker?

On their way to the barn they walked by a blue Honda CRV and a black Dodge Ram pickup with a license plate that read "CBJACK" and then the ranch house, its porch shaded by an overhead portico. On the porch an old black dog slept on a blanket next to a rocking chair. Hank pointed to the rocking chair. "That's where Jack Ryan used to sit. The old dog lays there waiting for him to return."

As they approached the barn a tall, lean woman stepped out of the wide doorway that revealed horse stalls below and a hayloft above. The woman walked out brushing straw from her short, red hair. A cowgirl, she wore jeans and a black western shirt, along with a fancy pair of Ranch Road boots. She also wore a shoulder holster with what looked like a Glock 9 mm tucked inside.

Fernando frowned. He felt like he'd entered an armed camp waiting for the command to attack.

"Mornin' Ruth," Hank said.

The woman jumped when she heard her name, startled. Apparently she hadn't noticed them.

"Jesus, Hank! You scared the daylights out of me!" she scolded Hank.

"Sorry, didn't mean to surprise you like that," Hank said. "How you holding up?"

Ruth shook her head. "The Luceros killed Morris, that's how. They owe me a son and I intend to get one. An eye for an eye. It's right there in the Bible."

"Well...I wouldn't put too much stock in that one line, Ruth. The Bible also says thou shalt not kill. One of the Ten Commandments."

"Don't matter to me," Ruth said. "They owe me a son. Who's this with you today?"

Hank introduced Fernando.

Fernando waved. He noticed the woman's brown, deeply wrinkled face. He figured her for a fifty-something, but she looked like she could be in her seventies. Too much sun.

Ruth frowned. "So what do you guys want, anyway? Did you come up the mountain to arrest those stinking Luceros?"

Hank laughed. "I wish we could do something to help you, Ruth. I really do. But so far it's just your word against theirs. We don't know who's shooting who or who's shooting first. It's he said versus he's dead."

"Yeah, so you keep saying," Ruth said, staring at Hank. "The law's never been a damn bit of help. So why are you here? What do you want now?"

"We need to talk to Jack Junior."

"What about?" she asked, suspicious.

"Well, about a woman who he's been having relations with at the Sagebrush Inn," Hank said. "Turns out that woman was murdered night before last."

She flashed them the Evil Eye. "Jack Junior goes into town to have a little fun. He's at that age where he needs to sow his oats. It gets lonely up here on the mountain for a young man. Why don't you just leave him alone?"

Before Hank could answer they heard the clatter of horse hooves approaching on the hard-packed dirt road coming down from the mountain. Then a horse came into view just beyond the corrals, a big roan with a mottled gray body and a reddish-brown head. The roan trotted around to the barn. When Cowboy Jack jumped off its back, the horse pawed the ground and shook its head, blowing loudly. Cowboy Jack tied the reins to a fence post and ambled over to where they stood. He looked like a young Paul Newman, clean-shaven and handsome as all get out. His white western hat was tipped back on his head. That and the smile on his face gave him a cocky appearance. He looked every bit like a ladies man.

"What's this all about?" Cowboy Jack asked. He glanced from his mother to Hank to Fernando.

"Well, son, we need to speak to you about Anne Lewis," Hank said, "the woman you had relations with at the Sagebrush two nights ago."

Cowboy Jack shrugged. "Yeah?"

"Thing is, she turned up dead yesterday morning. Appears someone drowned her in the swimming pool."

The mother sighed.

"Someone murdered her?" Cowboy Jack asked.

Hank nodded. He explained how she was found floating in the Sagebrush pool. "You'd had relations with Miss Lewis and you were at the Sagebrush the night she was murdered. Did you go to her room that night?"

"No," Cowboy Jack said calmly. "She ignored me, so I hooked up with someone else."

"Who would that be?" Hank asked.

"Bonnie somebody. I can't remember her last name. She works in the crew, doing lighting, I think."

Hank wrote the name down in his pocket notebook. "And this Bonnie will corroborate your story?"

Cowboy Jack threw his head back. "Yeah, why wouldn't she? It was a night she'll never forget."

The mother raised her hands. "That's enough for me. Don't want to hear any more," she said, walking off toward the house.

Fernando stepped forward. "What about afterwards? Did you stop by Anne Lewis' room or the swimming pool?"

"Oh, hell no, it was nearly morning by then, I needed to get home," Cowboy Jack said, bragging.

Fernando frowned, not impressed by the macho act.

Hank handed the young man one of his cards. "Okay, if you're telling the truth, you have nothing to worry about. That said, you'll have to come into the station for fingerprinting and a DNA sample. We're located on Lovato Place, the address on the card."

"Why's that? Why would I need to give you a DNA sample?"

"Because you're a suspect," Hank said. "You can come in voluntarily and give us a sample or I can arrest you and force you to give us a sample. Suit yourself."

"Arrest me?" Cowboy Jack asked. He stood frozen for a moment and then panicked, turning around and rushing for his horse. He reached for the rifle in his saddle scabbard.

Hank and Fernando immediately drew their weapons.

"Don't!" Hank barked. "Don't make me shoot you, son."

Cowboy Jack turned around slowly, staring at two drawn pistols. He'd lost his cocky attitude.

Hank frowned. "Tell you what. I'll give you until the day after tomorrow to come in. If you don't come in, I'll send a damn SWAT team out here to drag you in. Understand?"

Cowboy Jack glared at Hank and then nodded.

Hank motioned for Fernando to follow him. They walked back to the house and waved at Ruth, now sitting on the porch. She waved back from the rocker with the old dog at her feet.

Fernando followed Hank down the long driveway. Every so often he would glance over his shoulder to make sure that Cowboy Jack and Donnie weren't zeroing in on them with their rifles.

They squeezed around the gate again and were about to get into the cruiser when they heard a shot ring out. It pinged against the metal 'Ryan Ranch' sign overhead and ricocheted off into the mesa.

"Nice. Real friendly folks," Fernando said.

4

Hank's cell phone rang just as he turned right on Cabresto Canyon Road. He pulled off alongside the road and answered. "Roy? Okay. Are they sure? What about Ted Fisher's? No kidding. Okay, I'm on my way."

"What's up?" Fernando asked.

Hank looked in the mirror and then pulled back onto Cabresto. "Roy got the DNA results. Turns out the two condoms have different DNA-- neither of them Ted Fisher's. And so far Forensics hasn't found Fisher's DNA or fingerprints anywhere in Anne Lewis' room."

"I guess that lets Fisher off the hook," Fernando said. "Sort of."

Hank shrugged. "Listen, I have to be in court at one o'clock. Probably take most of the afternoon. Can you find this Bonnie character who Cowboy Jack says he spent the night with? He said she works in the crew doing lighting. See what she says about that night."

"Sure. I'll just have to find out where they're shooting today."

"Check with Roy," Hank said. "Someone with the movie dropped off a shooting schedule at the station, just in case we would need to provide traffic control or whatever."

As usual Hank drove a good twenty miles an hour over the speed limit, careening down the mountain and then turning left on Highway 522. He raced through Questa and Arroyo Hondo and didn't slow down until he reached the outskirts of Taos. They stopped for a quick lunch at Orlando's and then drove through Taos to the station on Lovato Place south of downtown.

Roy found the movie's shooting schedule while Hank gathered his papers and then left for the courthouse. "Here you go," Roy said, handing the schedule to Fernando. "Looks like they're here till the end of the week."

According to the schedule, the movie crew would be shooting at the historic Martinez Hacienda. "That's on Lower Ranchitos Road, a few long blocks west of the Plaza," Roy said.

Fernando nodded. "I'll find it."

But finding the Martinez Hacienda was easier said than done, Fernando discovered. He drove to the Plaza but got lost trying to find Ranchitos Road, which according to his map would take him to Lower Ranchitos Road. He finally found an entrance to Ranchitos on Camino de la Placita. As soon as he turned left on Lower Ranchitos he saw the Martinez Hacienda on the right side of the road, a monumental adobe structure surrounded by corrals and a stream that ran through its property. Adobe buttresses supported the thick walls of the massive structure that dated from 1804. A museum now, it was listed on the National Historic Register.

Fernando parked his Cherokee behind the line of movie trailers parked along Lower Ranchitos. He saw a number of the crew standing by the weathered wooden doors of the old hacienda. Must be shooting inside, he figured. So he walked up to a man holding a clipboard and introduced himself. "Can you help me? I'm looking for Bonnie--she works in lighting, I think."

"You must mean Bonnie Alvarez," he said, an older man wearing a Los Angeles Dodgers baseball cap and dressed all in denim. He pointed to one of the trailers. "She's over in that trailer with the open door."

"Much obliged," Fernando said. He walked to the trailer and knocked softly on the aluminum door.

"Come in, the door's open," a woman said.

Fernando stepped inside a trailer crowded with electronics and lighting equipment. He saw a thirty-something woman standing on a folding stepladder. She appeared to be sorting through a collection of lighting cables on an overhead shelf. She turned to face him, wearing faded jeans and a black T-shirt with what looked like either a Japanese or Chinese symbol in silver glitter on its front.

"Yes? What is it?"

Fernando realized he was staring at the woman. With a silver ring through one eyebrow and short blue hair, she was striking. A knock-out.

"I'd like to ask you some questions about Jack Ryan Junior," Fernando said and introduced himself. "He's a person of interest in the Anne Lewis murder. Are you familiar with Jack?"

Bonnie smiled. "You mean Cowboy Jack? Yes, I am familiar with him." She laughed.

"He says he was with you on the night Anne was murdered. Can you corroborate that?"

She climbed down from the folding ladder and sat on the top step. "Part of the night, yes. He was gone by morning."

"Do you have any idea what time he left your room?" Fernando asked.

She laughed. "I don't remember a thing. I was a totally satisfied woman."

He didn't know how to respond to that, so he laughed too. "Well, I'm glad you enjoyed yourself."

Bonnie nodded. "Oh yeah. He was just as good as Anne said he was."

"You said he was gone by morning, but can you be a little more specific," Fernando said. "Was it close to morning or more like the middle of the night?"

She sighed. "I think it was close to morning. I sort of remember him leaving. It seems like it was already getting light outside when he left."

"And you say Anne told you about him."

"Sure, we always shared our stories," she said. "Cowboy Jack comes every night looking for sex and usually doesn't have any trouble finding it. He's a hot item, a real lady pleaser."

Ignoring that, Fernando asked, "What about Anne Lewis? Did you see her that night? Did you see who she was with?"

"I saw her when we first arrived at the Cantina. She was talking to Cassie at the bar for maybe half an hour. Then she left, by herself. That was the last I saw of her."

Fernando handed her a card. "Okay. If you can think of anything else, give me a call."

She stood up and took his card. "Will do."

He stepped out of the trailer and lingered a few minutes in the drive, watching the actors going back and forth between their trailers and the Hacienda. He saw Cassie and Jacqueline and an actor he thought was the male lead, a muscular guy wrapped in a commando costume that made him look like he belonged to a SWAT team. Or a Marvel comic book.

None of the actors had time to stop and answer Fernando's questions, so he left. The only way he knew to get from the Martinez Hacienda to the sheriff's office was to backtrack to the Plaza and take Paseo del Pueblo Sur to Lovato Place. When he pulled into the parking lot the sun was already sinking in the western sky.

Sally, the dispatcher, greeted him as he walked into the office. "Hey, Fernando, I heard you were here earlier." I took the morning off to get a sonogram."

"Hi Sally," Fernando said. "I wondered where you were."

"Yeah, I had to get a sonogram," she said, patting her stomach, a small woman with a round face and high cheekbones, her long black hair falling to her shoulders in curls.

He realized she was pregnant. "Everything okay?"

"Yeah, except I have to pee every fifteen minutes."

Fernando laughed. "I remember Estelle saying the same thing." He looked around but didn't see Hank.

"No, Hank hasn't come back from the courthouse," Sally said. "I don't think he plans to return today. Roy's still here. You want me to call him?"

Fernando shook his head. "No, that's okay. You guys really are short-handed. The office looks like a damn ghost station."

"I know, Hank's had a hard time recruiting," Sally said. "We're up to four open positions now. Dave's so busy he hardly comes in. Luckily Roy helps with the paperwork."

Fernando nodded. "Okay, I'll see you tomorrow morning. Hopefully Hank will be back by then."

Calling it a day, he drove back to the Sagebrush and parked in front. He called Estelle first thing and told her he wouldn't be home for at least another day. Then he walked next door to the Guadalajara Grill for dinner. By the time he made it back to the Sagebrush the movie trailers were already parked in the rear of the lot. Inside he found most of the actors and crew milling around the Cantina or restaurant areas. He caught a glimpse of Cassie and Jacqueline but not Cowboy Jack. Just to be sure he hung out in the hallway for a while looking for Cowboy Jack. Finally he gave up and walked back to his courtyard room.

Bored, Fernando turned on the television and lay down on the nearest bed. He watched a few innings of a Colorado Rockies baseball game before falling into a deep sleep.

He woke up suddenly to the sound of pounding on his door: Bam! Bam!

"Help! Help me, please!" someone yelled outside in the hallway. A woman's voice.

Fernando climbed out of bed, groggy. He looked around for his pants and then realized he hadn't taken them off before climbing into bed. He stumbled to the door and threw it open.

"Mister Lopez, please, help me!" an hysterical Cassie pleaded. Her blond hair was tousled and her shirt and short skirt in disarray. She tried to force her way into his room but Fernando resisted.

"What's the matter?" he asked.

"Ted. He tried to rape me! He's grabbing me all over and won't leave me alone."

Just then Ted Fisher appeared at the end of the hallway. "Ah-hah, there you are," he said, spying Cassie. He looked as disheveled as Cassie, with his white shirt hanging out of his jeans. He walked unsteadily toward them.

When he saw Fisher approaching, Fernando moved aside and let Cassie enter his room.

"Come back, Cassie," Fisher pleaded and tried to get around Fernando, who stood his ground.

Fernando folded his arms across his chest and blocked the doorway.

"What are you doing?" Fisher asked. "Get outta my way."

"Leave her alone," Fernando said.

Fisher looked nonplused, then angry. Clearly he was a man used to getting his way. "Do you know who I am? I'm the fucking executive producer of this movie, now get out of my way."

Fernando didn't move. He shook his head. "No. Go back to your room at the Taos Inn. You want me to call you a cab?"

Fisher stared at him incredulously. He balled his fists, swaying side to side. "No, I don't want you to call me a fucking cab!"

For a moment Fernando thought Fisher would try to punch him, but even drunk the man was smarter than that. Fisher backed away slowly, looking around the hall to make sure he hadn't created a public spectacle. He hadn't. The dark hallway was empty now.

Fernando watched Fisher walk away and then went back into his room. He shut and locked the door behind him.

"Thank you!" Cassie said and threw her arms around him. She too smelled like booze.

"So what happened?" Fernando asked.

She looked offended. "Nothing happened, if that's what you mean."

She brushed the hair out of her eyes and looked around the room, spotting the stuffed chair near the window. She moved over to the chair and helped herself.

"No, I ran into him at the bar and we had a few drinks," Cassie said, composing herself. "I said goodnight, but he followed me to my room and forced his way in. Then he grabbed me and started kissing me. Trying to pull off my clothes. I screamed but he wouldn't stop. Finally I told him I had to go to the bathroom for a minute. Instead, I ran out of the room and left him on the bed. I came here because I remembered you were staying in this room."

Fernando nodded.

"He's a brute," Cassie said. "No wonder Anne and those other women are suing him."

"So I hear," Fernando said.

"You don't mind if I stay here tonight, do you? I'm totally exhausted. I'll take that other bed." Cassie moved over to the bed that hadn't been slept in and jumped on the mattress. She bounced on the mattress a few times and then stared at him. "What do you say?"

He laughed. "Well then...why don't you help yourself."

Cassie missed his sarcasm. "Yeah, but I'm not taking my clothes off," she said, giving him a firm look. "I mean it!"

He threw up his hands in defeat.

"And don't you take your clothes off either," she said, switching off the light on her nightstand and pulling the bedcovers over her short dress.

Fernando followed her orders.

5

Fernando dreamed of sleeping next to Cassie. He could smell her perfume and feel her skin, warm and soft to the touch. She'd slipped into his bed in the middle of the night to cuddle. He knew he shouldn't touch her, but his body told him otherwise. When he heard a clicking sound he thought Cassie had gone to the bathroom. Waiting for her to return seemed to take forever, until he heard another clicking sound that brought him to the surface of consciousness. This click sounded like the door to his room opening and then closing.

Fernando cracked open an eye and saw Cassie coming into the room holding two large coffees in a cardboard tray. She fumbled with the keycard and the coffees, spilling a little coffee on the carpet. She smiled when she saw he was awake and kicked the door closed behind her.

"Time to wake up, sleepy head," she said, placing the coffees on the desk across the room. She was fully dressed, wearing white slacks and a blue sweater. In the morning light she looked even more attractive than he remembered. No wonder he'd dreamed about sleeping with her.

He rubbed the sleep out of his eyes. "How'd you get back in?"

"Oh, I took one of the keycards on the desk," she said, matter-of-factly. "I didn't think you'd mind. So how do you like your coffee? Black, or with some cream and sugar?"

Fernando grunted. "Dump everything in, cream and sugar," he said. "How long have you been up?"

"I had to get an early start. We have an eight o'clock shoot at the Martinez Hacienda again today."

He sat up in bed and accepted one of the steaming hot coffees from her. "Thanks. I have a hard time waking up. In case you haven't noticed."

Cassie laughed. "So I see."

"Did you sleep okay? I mean, with your clothes on and all...and a strange man in the next bed?"

"I did, actually," she said. "When I'm away from home I usually have a hard time sleeping, but the beds in this new wing of the Sagebrush are surprisingly comfortable. I would come here again. And...the man sleeping in the next bed was a true gentleman."

Fernando smiled. He was both amused and annoyed at how chipper she was this early in the morning.

Over coffee Cassie chatted nonstop about the day's shooting schedule and the convoluted storyline, which went something like this: their muscle-bound commando hero learns from a dying 105-year-old Taoseño that one particular witch, or *bruja*, knows who has the secret knowledge to defeat the hordes of awakened dead stalking the countryside. The witch lives in a secret hiding place at the Martinez Hacienda and can only be conjured up by a secret incantation known only by a few ancient members of the Taos Penitente Brotherhood, of which the 105-year-old is a member. So armed with the secret incantation, thanks to the 105-year-old Taoseño, their hero enters the Martinez Hacienda, conjures the *bruja*, and learns who has the secret of defeating the awakened dead who are ravaging and killing the good citizens of Taos.

"So who has the secret? And what is the secret?" Fernando asked, vaguely interested.

Cassie shook her head. "We haven't gotten that far yet. I think it has something to do with a secret herb found on the banks of Blue Lake--the holy lake belonging to Taos Pueblo--that can only be identified by a particular Taos Pueblo medicine man who's the keeper of the secret. Totally preposterous."

"Hmmm, lotta secrets in that scenario," he said.

She laughed, and then chatted cheerfully about their macho hero, a former professional wrestler who she sort of liked even though he wasn't very smart and had to be constantly reminded of his lines, but she couldn't complain because this was her first big break and she had to take advantage of every opportunity. "Yeah, he's a big lunkhead," Cassie said.

Fernando kept nodding, unused to people who talked this much and this fast. Her cheerfulness could be downright irritating. He said nothing, he only listened.

Finally Cassie ran out of gas. She grabbed her purse and what was left of her coffee and said, "See you later."

Fernando watched her walk out the door, noticing she hadn't left the extra keycard to his door on the desk. What was that all about? Was she planning to return this evening?

After he finished his coffee Fernando splashed water on his face and changed clothes. Next he went to the Sagebrush Grill for breakfast, his usual order of huevos rancheros. Finally he drove down the Paseo to Lovato Place and pulled into the parking lot of the sheriff's office next to a beat-up Chevy pickup. The pickup had a Questa High School sticker on its bumper. The truck was parked across the sidewalk, partially blocking the front door.

Looked like Trouble.

Fernando walked around the pickup to the door. As soon as he stepped inside he knew something was amiss. He saw Sally and Hank hovering over a young girl in Hank's office in back. It looked like the two of them were trying to comfort the girl, who appeared to be weeping. What now? Had someone else been shot on Cabresto Canyon Road? Either a Ryan or a Lucero?

Hank spotted Fernando and waved him back to the office. Even though Fernando would rather not join them, he went anyway. Hank rolled his eyes and pointed to the young girl, who looked like a teenager with shoulder length brown hair and a bad complexion. She wore jeans and a Questa High T-shirt and was bawling like a baby. Tears were streaming down her face.

"This here's Rosalia Lucero," Hank said to Fernando. "She's worried about her two brothers, Armando and Tony. Someone ambushed Armando yesterday evening and tried to kill him. Probably Cowboy Jack."

Rosalia, who had a wad of tissues in her hand, reached for another and dabbed at her eyes. One look at Fernando and she burst out crying again. "Please...you've gotta help me...this is the second time Armando's been shot at...they're gonna kill him like they killed my daddy...why can't you stop them...you're the sheriff...you're supposed to prevent stuff like this from happening...why can't you arrest Jack Junior before he kills my brothers? Put him in jail!"

Hank straightened up and tried to remain cool, calm, and collected. He introduced Fernando. "Rosalia, this is Fernando Lopez. He's a former detective down in Santa Fe. He's helping us out for a bit."

Rosalia sobbed into her wad of tissues, paying no attention to Fernando.

"Now, I understand your frustration," Hank said. "But the thing is, Armando shot and killed Morris Ryan."

Rosalia turned to face Hank, furious. "That's only because Morris killed my daddy!"

"Yes, and Morris killed your daddy because your daddy shot and killed his daddy," Hank responded. "Don't you see? This whole cycle of violence has to stop. Right now. Before it's too late. Or the whole lot of you will be killed."

"I know, I know," Rosalia continued to sob. "That's what I tell them, but my brothers won't listen. And mama, she doesn't speak any more, ever since my daddy died. She stays inside wearing her black dress and moves around the house like a ghost. She never goes out. She's just...I don't know...she's just given up."

Hank sighed. He glanced at Fernando and then said, "Okay. All right. I'll go out and talk to them again. I don't know what good it'll do, since they haven't listened to me up till now, but I'll give it another shot."

Rosalia looked up at Hank with tears in her eyes. "*Muchas gracias*! I appreciate your help. Whatever you can do."

"Tell you what, we'll follow you back to the ranch," Hank said. "That way your brothers won't shoot us."

Rosalia grinned.

So the three of them left together, leaving Sally to mind the station by herself. Hank and Fernando waited until Rosalia moved her pickup from the sidewalk and then walked to Hank's cruiser. Rosalia drove slowly, which drove Hank crazy because he liked to drive fast. Impatiently tapping on the steering wheel and from time to time nearly running into the back of Rosalia's pickup, Hank followed her through Taos and then north on Highway 522. In Questa they turned right at the visitor center and drove up Cabresto Canyon Road to the unmarked gravel road that led to both the Ryan and Lucero ranches.

When the road dead-ended at the T, Rosalia turned right into the Lucero Ranch, which unlike the Ryan ranch didn't have a gate. They drove by a small cornfield with a red-garbed scarecrow in the middle that looked so real Fernando did a double take. It looked like a human figure, crucified.

Hank gave the pickup a little more room once they entered the ranch proper. He didn't want the Lucero family to think he was chasing Rosalia. The Lucero Ranch was smaller and older and further up the mountain than the Ryan's, with only a small adobe house and a weathered wooden barn surrounded by corrals. The corrals extended all the way to the edge of the foothills, covered with pine and piñon trees. A narrow animal trail could be seen winding into the foothills and up the mountain. From a distance the trail looked like a ribbon.

Rosalia parked near the house alongside a new model Jeep Wrangler and an old Chevy Blazer, its blue paint faded to splotches by the intense New Mexico sun. She climbed out of her pickup and waited for them.

Hank parked some distance from the pickup, just in case they had to make a fast exit. They didn't know the whereabouts of the Lucero boys or if the two brothers were armed. "This will give us some space to manoeuver," Hank said.

Fernando nodded, and the two of them stepped out of the cruiser.

Fernando pointed to the barn, where one of the brothers had poked his head out of the door to check on their visitors. "Up there. One of them just stuck his head out of the barn door."

"Hmmm...looks like Tony, the younger brother," Hank said.

Rosalia joined them. "You'll need to talk to Armando. He and Tony are fixing a stall in the barn. Like I said, mama isn't speaking."

"Okay, darlin'. Lead the way," Hank said.

Hank and Fernando followed her to the barn, a gray, weathered structure with a loft and a rusted tin roof. Several horses whinnied as they approached the corrals. One, a large black stallion, snorted and pawed the ground.

"Not even the horses are glad to see us," Fernando joked.

"Wait till you meet Armando," Hank said.

The sound of hammering came from inside the barn.

As they approached the younger brother stepped out of the barn to meet them. Tony was carrying a deer rifle. An old deer rifle.

Fernando smelled the richly fragrant mixture of hay, straw, and horseshit coming from the barn. The smell brought back memories of his grandparents' ranch in the Pecos. He'd spent a good part of his youth on their ranch, tending their horses and lazing around their barn. Later, in high school, he and some of his buddies would hide out in the barn and smoke weed. Smoke from their weed was the one thing that covered the rank smell of the barn.

"I brought the sheriff," Rosalia said to her brother.

"Why'd you do that? Now Armando's gonna be pissed," Tony said and ducked back into the barn.

They followed Tony inside the barn, finding Armando repairing a stall. Armando stopped when he saw Hank enter, setting his hammer down on a makeshift work table made out of planks and two saw horses. A short, powerfully built man with huge shoulders and a military crew cut, he frowned and mumbled something in Spanish under his breath.

"What's up, Armando?" Hank asked.

Armando shook his head. "Trying to fix this stall. Horse got spooked by either a bobcat or mountain lion last night. Kicked out the gate."

"Better shut the barn doors," Hank said.

"They'll come in through the loft if they're hungry enough," Armando said and then stared at Hank. "So what brings you out here?"

"Your sister came in to talk to us this morning. She's worried about you and Tony. This feud's got to stop, Armando. You got to stop killing each other."

Armando frowned. "Tell that to Jack Junior. He took a shot at me yesterday evening up past the corrals. Hit the fence post I was working on. If I'd a had my rifle, I would have killed him right then. It won't happen again."

"What you're doing is against the law, Armando," Hank said. "And it's against every law in the Good Book. Enough is enough. You're the one who caused this latest round of killing when you shot Morris Ryan. Stop now before you lose your entire family."

"Why? Morris killed my daddy!" Armando shot back. "I had to kill him. An eye for an eye, that's how it works."

Hank shook his head. "Yeah, I keep hearing that up here...but listen, Morris killed your daddy because your daddy killed his daddy, goddamnit. Why can't you get that in your head? Now you've gone and killed Morris, the Ryans oldest son, so I suppose they're gonna have to kill you. Where does it stop? With Tony? Rosalia? Is that what you want?"

"It stops when I kill Jack Junior before he kills me," Armando said.

"No!" Hank shouted in Armando's face. "If you kill Jack Junior, Donnie Ryan will try to kill you."

"Let him try," Armando said.

"The killing stops when all of you make amends and stop killing each other, Ryans and Luceros both. Don't you understand?"

Armando spit on the straw covered floor. "Well, go tell that to the Ryans, then."

"That's where I'm headed now!" Hank bellowed. He turned around and walked angrily out of the barn. Seeing Rosalia, he stopped and said, "I can't talk any sense into your dumbass brother!"

Fernando followed Hank back to the cruiser. On the way he noticed Isabel, the mother, watching from inside the house. She stood inside the screen door, dressed entirely in black, her face shrouded by a dark veil. She watched them walk across the yard and then seemed to float away into the interior of the house. Like a ghost, Rosalia had said. She moved around the house like a ghost.

Hank was too busy cursing to notice Isabel. The big man climbed into the cruiser and fired the engine, hardly waiting for Fernando to scramble into the passenger's seat before he roared off, leaving a trail of dust behind.

"See what I mean?" Hank snapped. "It's hopeless. Hell, I don't know, maybe it's better to let them all kill each other. Give a man a gun and he has to kill something. Doesn't say much for the human race, does it?"

Fernando laughed. "No, it doesn't. Not the male of the species anyway."

Hank drove to the T at the end of the driveway and continued on into the Ryan Ranch. This time they found the gate wide open, an invitation to enter. So Hank continued on up to the make-shift bunker on the way to the house. Once again Donnie greeted them with his rifle.

Hank slammed on the brakes and stopped in a cloud of dust. He climbed out of the cruiser and barked, "Put that damn thing away! You're gonna hurt someone."

The kid was taken aback. Wearing shorts and a Nike T-shirt, he looked like he should be frolicking on some playground instead of playing sentry. He made the mistake of pointing the gun at Hank.

"Are you deaf?" Hank bellowed. "I told you to put that goddamn gun away!"

For a big man, Hank moved fast. He was on top of Donnie before the kid knew what hit him. Hank grabbed the rifle out of Donnie's hands and pushed the kid over on his nearly bare ass. Donnie just sat there in his ridiculous shorts staring up at the raging bear standing over him.

Hank emptied the rifle's chamber and tossed the shells as far as he could. Then he took the gun by its barrel and bashed it against the adobe bricks. Sand and chunks of adobe exploded around them as the big man continued to smash the gun over and over on the bricks until it came apart in his hands.

Donnie finally found his tongue. "I was just protecting our ranch, sheriff," he whined.

Hank frowned. "The hell you say! Your daddy should have taught you some manners. Why aren't you in school, doing something productive."

"It's summer, sheriff--my high school's on break," Donnie pleaded. "I'm helping out on the ranch."

"Doing what? Threatening people who come calling?"

Donnie did not respond.

Hank sighed, trying to shake off his anger. "Now where's Jack Junior? He has to stop this killing. All of you do."

"Jack? He just left. He went into town to give you a DNA sample, like you wanted."

"Figures," Hank said, looking around. "Okay. I'll try to catch him at the office. You tell him if he doesn't stop taking potshots at Armando Lucero, I'm gonna come back here and arrest him and maybe you too for attempted murder. Lock you both up and throw away the key. Got it?"

"But Armando killed Morris," Donnie said.

"Enough! I don't want to hear any more about who killed who because I don't give a damn," Hank said, turning to Fernando. "You got anything to add?"

"I got nothing," Fernando said. "You pretty much said it all."

Wide-eyed, mouth hanging open, Donnie watched them walk back to the cruiser without saying a word.

6

Sally stood behind the front counter when Fernando and Hank walked into the sheriff's office. She checked her watch and shook her head. "Darn, you just missed Jack Junior," she said. "He stopped in earlier to give us a DNA sample. Just left not fifteen minutes ago."

"Well, shit," Hank said. "Now I'm gonna have to drive back to Questa. I need to read that boy the riot act. Maybe I'll arrest his ass just for making me drive all the way back there."

Fernando agreed. "That's probably the only way you'll stop him from trying to shoot Armando."

Hank grumbled and walked back into his office.

Fernando decided to check out the scene at the Sagebrush. Hank could deal with Cowboy Jack, if he could ever catch up with him. He told Sally where he would be and then headed out the door. He climbed into his Cherokee and sat there thinking for a few moments. He considered returning home to Santa Fe until some new leads turned up in the Anne Lewis investigation. Then again, he knew Hank was occupied with the ongoing feud in Questa and didn't have a lot of time to pursue Anne's killer. Which more or less left it up to him. Whether he liked it or not.

Unable to make up his mind, Fernando drove slowly to the Sagebrush and parked out front, as usual. The movie vans and trailers had already left for the day's shoot, leaving the parking lot nearly empty. He ate an early lunch in the restaurant and then walked down the long hallway to his room intending to rest for a few minutes before heading out to wherever the crew was shooting. Stepping into the room he noticed a bright red suitcase lying on the second bed, the bed Cassie had slept in last night. What now? Was the woman moving in with him? Sure enough, the tag on the suitcase read Cassie Jenkins.

Suddenly his cell phone rang.

"Lopez," he answered, fumbling with the phone.

"Mister Lopez, this is Bonnie getting back to you."

Fernando tried to place the name.

"You gave me a card and asked me to call if I remembered anything more about Anne and Cowboy Jack," the woman said. "Bonnie, the lighting tech?"

That jogged his memory. "Yes, thanks for calling back."

"I'm on a short lunch break," she said. "We're downtown shooting on Ledoux Street, so I wondered if I could meet you on the Plaza?"

"Sure, I can come right down."

"I'll be on a bench near the bandstand," she said and clicked off.

He looked again at Cassie's suitcase and then said to hell with it. He would worry about that when he got back.

Back in the Cherokee, he took the Paseo into town and turned left into the Plaza area. He found a precious parking space near Mountain Outfitters and plugged his meter, giving himself a good hour and a half, in case he needed it.

He spotted Bonnie sitting on a bench by herself. She looked as striking as before, even with her short blue hair. She wore slacks today and a low-cut silk shirt that complemented her curves. She waved at him to get his attention.

Fernando crossed the street and walked across the Plaza to her bench, which was directly across the street from the Taos La Fonda. "Didn't expect to hear from you so soon."

Bonnie smiled. "Yeah, actually I remembered something Cowboy Jack said that I probably should have told you earlier. It might not be important, but I thought you should know."

"What's that?" he asked, sitting on the bench.

"Well...it's about Cowboy Jack on the night we hooked up," Bonnie said, hesitating as though embarrassed by what she had to say. "When things were getting hot and heavy, he asked if he could bring in a friend to join us."

"A friend," Fernando repeated. "You mean like a threesome?"

"Yeah. Exactly. I told him no, I like my coupling one on one."

"Do you have any idea who his friend might be?"

She shook her head. "None."

Fernando thought about this for a moment. "Well, clearly he comes to the Sagebrush to pick up women. When you see him in the Cantina, is he by himself, or is he with other people?"

She shrugged. "He's usually with one or two other young guys. I think. Sometimes it's hard to tell who's with whom. That bar gets crowded fast, especially on nights they have music."

Fernando nodded, thinking out loud. "So one of these guys who came with Jack could be Anne's killer. As well as someone working on the movie, of course."

Bonnie did not respond.

"Tell me," Fernando said. "Are there any Don Juans among the movie crowd that like to bed multiple women? You referred to Cowboy Jack as a 'hot item.' Are there any other 'hot item' guys among the cast or crew?"

Bonnie laughed. "Slim pickings, I'm afraid. The only guy who even thinks he's a ladies man is Trevor Bowen, the male lead. He's a big hunk of a guy, thinks he's real macho."

"The guy strutting around in the commando suit?"

"Exactly," Bonnie said. "He's bedded most of the women in the cast by now. He looks like hot stuff, so all the ladies try him once."

"Just once?"

"One time only, thank you," Bonnie said. "He's a terrible lover. Rough, impatient, selfish, you name it. When he's done, he's done and you can finish on your own. You know what I mean?"

Fernando nodded. "Had Anne slept with him too?"

"Of course, but only once as far as I know. Like I said, he's a terrible lover. If you're a self-respecting woman, you don't go back for seconds with a preening, self-absorbed Neanderthal like Trevor."

"Can he get violent?" Fernando asked. "If Anne rejected him, could he have gotten violent with her?"

Bonnie shrugged. "I don't know, maybe. He's dumb as a post, clumsy and way too rough with women, so maybe."

"What about the director? He looks like a ladies' man," Fernando said.

"José? No way. He's gay," she said, checking her watch. "Sorry, I have to get back. They're gonna start shooting in a few minutes."

Fernando waved and then watched her walk across the Plaza and disappear into the crowd on Teresina Lane. He lingered on the bench, reflecting on what Bonnie had told him. He added more possibilities to his list of suspects--Cowboy Jack's friend, or friends, and Trevor Bowen. While he brooded, he noticed two men standing out front of the Taos La Fonda Hotel looking directly at him. One of them gestured wildly with his hands while the other listened. He took a closer look and recognized both of them: the director, José Sousa, and none other than Ted Fisher, the executive producer. Staring at him.

When they noticed Fernando staring back at them, the two men stopped talking and walked away. They followed Bonnie.

Curious, Fernando followed them down Teresina Lane, making sure to keep a safe distance. They crossed Camino de la Placita to Ledoux Street, which was closed off at its entrance to accommodate the movie shoot. The two men entered a row of trailers and disappeared from view.

Fernando crossed Camino de la Placita and stopped in front of the metal barricades. Movie trailers blocked his view, so he walked into the parking lot of the Italian restaurant at the mouth of Ledoux Street, one of the artistic centers of Taos. He found a seat on a stone retaining wall at the edge of the property. From there he could see most of Ledoux Street, including camera crews getting ready to shoot down by the Harwood Museum. The colorful street presented a smorgasbord of brightly colored murals and sculptures, including a huge fish next to the Harwood.

As he watched, the scene unfolded before him.

Someone called out "action." On cue a small car came careening up the street, swerving from one side of the street to the other. Finally the car slammed into a rubberized wall painted adobe brown and made to look like the side of an adobe building. Suddenly Jacqueline Bonet, the heroine of the movie, climbed out of the car and staggered away gamely. She wore a skimpy dress that revealed nearly as much as it concealed. Just then a horde of dirty, discolored awakened dead wearing tattered rags appeared on the street chasing her. She screamed and ran madly toward a dark alley at the end of the street.

Fernando watched, waiting to see if the horde of awakened dead would overtake Jacqueline and either rip off her remaining clothes or eat her, whatever the awakened dead supposedly did, he had no idea. Instead a black motorcycle roared out of the alley and spun to a stop just long enough for Jacqueline to jump on the back. Gripping the handlebars was none other than the movie's muscle-bound hero, Trevor Bowen. Wearing a flaming red helmet, Bowen also wore a skin-tight commando costume designed to show off his bulges fore and aft. Bowen revved the engine and shot off across Ledoux Street. The motorcycle disappeared into the alley on the other side of the street, leaving the throng of awakened dead howling like a pack of werewolves.

Someone yelled "Cut" and moments later the motorcycle appeared on Ledoux Street without Jacqueline on back. She walked out of the alley a few minutes later without even glancing at Bowen, still straddling the motorcycle. Bowen held out his arms as if to ask what the problem was, but she turned her head and ignored him, walking directly to her trailer without looking back. From all signs there was no love lost between the two lead actors.

Fernando left shortly after the shooting stopped. He walked back to his Cherokee and drove to the Sagebrush. A late afternoon crowd had started to form in the Cantina, so he decided to join them. Happy hour came early in the Land of Enchantment, as New Mexicans liked to refer to their state. He found an empty table near the front door, where he had a clear view of the hallway in case Trevor Bowen happened to appear. He had some questions for Bowen, based on the information provided by Bonnie Alvarez about his sexual prowess, or lack thereof.

The bartender spotted him across the room and came over to his table. "What can I get you?" he asked, a wizened little man with a pointed goatee who he'd talked to last night.

"Modelo draft," Fernando said. "Same old, same old."

"You got it," the bartender said and returned shortly with a frosted glass of Modelo. "Couple of guys were asking about you earlier."

"Yeah? Who would that be?"

The bartender shook his head. He started to speak and then stopped and pointed out in the hallway. "There they are."

Fernando saw Ted Fisher talking to a thin well-tanned man wearing an exquisitely tailored blue suit that made him look like a real dandy. The suit also made him stand out like a sore thumb in a cowboy town like Taos. The man had slicked back black hair and a teethy smile, teeth as white as porcelain. A lawyer, no question about it. An L.A. lawyer.

Fisher pointed at Fernando and then walked off down the hallway. The fancy, well-dressed dude walked a beeline to Fernando's table.

"Hi there," the man said. "I'm Richard Rosenthal, one of the lawyers representing The Awakened Dead."

Fernando laughed. "Sounds like you're representing dead people."

Rosenthal blushed. "No, I mean I'm representing the producers of the movie. They're...well, they're not dead."

Fernando couldn't resist. "You mean they're the undead."

"Well, let's just call them the living," Rosenthal said, nonplussed by the linguistic confusion.

"Gets confusing, doesn't it," Fernando said. "What can I do for you?"

Rosenthal pulled out a chair. "Do you mind if I sit down?"

Fernando waved his hand. "Help yourself."

"Thank you," Rosenthal said, and took a seat across from Fernando. "Actually I'm here to talk business. I understand you're a former detective in the Santa Fe Police Department. Well, it so happens that we're looking for someone to take charge of security on the movie set. I'm sure you're aware of the tragic death of Anne Lewis, one of our cast members."

Fernando stopped him there. "Murder, you mean."

"Yes, of course. Anyway, to cut to the chase, we wanted to offer you the position. It would only be for a week or two. We should be done shooting by then. You could even bring in someone to work under you, if you wished. We thought of you first, since you're already staying in the hotel."

Fernando smelled a rat. He wasn't disappointed.

When Fernando didn't respond, Rosenthal continued. "We don't have unlimited funds, but we would be willing to give you a generous stipend. The only thing we would need is for you to sign a nondisclosure agreement. Standard procedure."

"A nondisclosure agreement?" Fernando asked.

Rosenthal nodded. "Agreeing not do discuss or disclose anything that's happened here during the movie shoot."

"Hah! So that's your play!" Fernando said. "You want to keep me quiet about the night Fisher attacked Cassie."

Rosenthal looked disappointed. "Well, I would hardly call it an attack. A disagreement, maybe. Certainly the incident was consensual."

"Not true, it wasn't consensual. If Fisher told you that, he's lying. You'd think he'd be more cautious since he's already accused of sexually assaulting three other women, one of whom was just murdered here at the Sagebrush, a little too conveniently for him."

"Well...." Rosenthal began but then stopped.

"So my answer is no," Fernando said. "And if Cassie wants me to testify on her behalf, I'll do it. Now take a hike."

With a haughty, disgusted expression on his face, Rosenthal stood and looked down at Fernando. "Here's a card if you change your mind--I'll be in town until the end of the week," he said and walked away.

Fernando listened to the echo of footsteps on the wooden floor as Rosenthal disappeared down the hallway.

Alone, Fernando finished his Modelo and ordered another. Later he drove into town to meet Hank for Dinner at Michael's Kitchen. Afterwards they went to the Taos Inn for drinks and to listen to a classical guitarist perform. It was nearly 10 p.m. by the time he returned to the Sagebrush. He called Estelle and gave her an update and then went to bed.

Sometime later he heard the door to his room open. He cracked his eyes open just wide enough to see Cassie enter and close the door softly behind her. He watched as she tip-toed into the bathroom, did her business, and then came back into the bedroom. She took something out of her suitcase and then placed the suitcase on the floor. Next she stripped off her clothes and then put on pajamas. Finished, she looked over at his bed, as if deciding whether to crawl in with him. She didn't. Instead, she pulled the bedclothes down on the second bed and climbed in with a big sigh.

Like it or not, he had a roommate.

7

"Wake up, sleepy head," a woman's voice whispered in his ear. "It's already past eight."

Fernando opened his eyes and saw Cassie's smiling face leaning over him. Half asleep, he reached up and grabbed her, pulling her into the bed and kissing her. She kissed him back and then hugged him tight. He felt her nipples harden through the thin silk pajamas. Then he realized what he was doing and stopped abruptly. Now that he was awake, he felt remorseful.

Should he apologize?

When Fernando released her, Cassie climbed out of bed and smiled. "Why, Mister Lopez, you're a gentleman."

Fernando laughed. "Just my luck."

She bent over and kissed him on the forehead. "Well, I won't tempt you anymore. My scenes are all finished so I'm flying back to L.A. this evening. I have to catch a six o'clock flight at the Albuquerque airport. I'll take an afternoon shuttle from the Sagebrush."

Fernando didn't know what to say so he said nothing.

"Anyway, thanks for keeping me safe. I'm in communication with the lawyer representing Anne and the other women who were sexually assaulted by Ted Fisher. I plan to testify."

"Good for you. Let's hope he gets what he deserves."

He sat up in bed and watched Cassie get dressed. She settled on a navy blue suit with a tight white blouse. Afterwards she primped in the bathroom for a good half hour before reappearing. Then she repacked her suitcase and placed it on the bed. "I'll be back for my suitcase later," she said, waving on her way out of the room. Just like that she was gone.

Alone, Fernando felt abandoned. He knew that was crazy. Cassie meant nothing to him, really. He would never see her again. And yet he still felt abandoned.

This entire episode with Cassie confused him to no end. He should know better at his age. So he climbed out of bed and did the sensible thing--he brewed himself a cup of coffee and tried to forgot about it.

He took his time, still feeling a little fuzzy from last night's drinks at the Taos Inn. Hank was a bad influence. The big man could drink all night. He couldn't.

Fernando used the bathroom and made himself presentable. He didn't like what he saw in the mirror: a deeply wrinkled face with dark circles under the eyes and salt and pepper hair. More salt than pepper every time he looked.

Once dressed, his first order of business was breakfast. He hoped to find Trevor Bowen in the restaurant so he didn't have to track him down and confront him on the movie set. He needed to know if Bowen was with Anne Lewis on the night she was murdered.

So after hanging the "Do Not Disturb" sign on his door, he headed down the dark hallway. He didn't see a soul, only dirty trays from room service outside several doors on his way to the restaurant. Nearing the end of the hallway he heard footsteps behind him. The footsteps seem to grow louder, alarming him.

Fernando turned to see who was there. Too late.

He glimpsed an object coming toward him out of the corner of his eye. Suddenly something hard hit him on the side of his head. A flash of pain and bright light sent him reeling to the floor.

Into the darkness.

Sirens woke him sometime later. He felt a searing pain in the back of his head and a sticky wetness on the left side of his face and neck. His body felt heavy, as though it were made of cement.

He tried to move but a medic held his arm tight. Slowly the realization came that he was riding in an ambulance on his way to a hospital. Not what he wanted. If they would only unstrap him he would be just fine. He struggled against the straps that held him on the stretcher. To no avail.

"What happened?" Fernando managed to ask weakly.

"Someone clobbered you, fella," the medic said. "Did you get into a fight or something?"

Fernando shook his head, feeling the blood squish around his neck. He didn't remember a fight, only walking down the dark hallway and hearing someone following him.

The ambulance pulled into the nearby Holy Cross Hospital within minutes. The medic jumped out the back, and within seconds he was wheeled into the Emergency Room.

Nurses descended on him like a pack of witches performing their macabre rites. IVs, inoculations, and blood tests followed. After cleaning and dressing his head, they hooked him up to beeping machines that measured his pulse, blood pressure, and oxygen levels.

By then Fernando was fully awake and feeling prickly. "Hey--I haven't had breakfast yet," he said.

They ignored him. Instead, they wheeled him down to Radiology for a CT-Scan of his noggin and then wheeled him back to the Emergency Room.

"How's your head?" one of the male nurses asked.

"Hurts like hell, what do you think," he snapped. "Give me two Tylenol and a glass of water."

"Wait a minute. I might be able to give you something stronger as soon as your CT results come in."

"I don't want anything stronger," Fernando said. "I'll be fine. I just need a couple of Tylenol."

After that the nurse abandoned him and went back to the nurses station to confer with the rest of the team. Fernando waited, his mouth parched and his head pounding, until the nurse returned with his Tylenol. Then the nurse returned again with insurance forms for him to fill out, which he hadn't been able to do earlier. He wanted breakfast; they gave him insurance forms.

Eventually a pale young woman wearing a doctor's white coat came over to his gurney. She peered over her heavy glasses and introduced herself as Doctor Turner. "Mister Lopez--tell me if you need something stronger than the Tylenol--we have your CT results now," she said. "You're a lucky man. There's no intracranial hemorrhage or acute infarct, no hydrocephalus or underlying fracture. Just a scalp hematoma, which should heal in time. The only serious problem the CT showed was mild-to-moderate global cerebral volume loss, suggestive of chronic microvascular disease. That's not unusual for a man your age."

"For a man my age? What's that supposed to mean?" Fernando asked.

The doctor laughed. "Well, for a man in his sixties. We all loose cerebral matter as we age. There's nothing unusual about that."

Fernando did not see the humor. "Thanks a lot, doc. Now when can I get out of here?"

"We'll keep you here another hour or so, just to be on the safe side," she said, taking the IV out of Fernando's arm and replacing it with a band aid. "But hey, you have a visitor out front. I'll send him back."

Hoping for Cassie, he heard instead Hank's booming voice in the waiting room. Moments later Hank burst into his cubicle and removed his black Stetson, as if he were standing for the National Anthem or, more appropriately, paying his last respects at a funeral. "Well, well, what have we here?" Hank said. "What in the hell happened to you?"

"Somebody brained me from behind in the hallway of the Sagebrush. Next thing I know I'm in a damned ambulance on my way here."

Hank examined the bandage on the left side of Fernando's head. "How's it feel?"

"Hurts like a motherfucker," Fernando said.

"Didn't they give you any opioids?" Hank asked.

"No, just Tylenol."

Hank shook his head. "Well, shit, do you have any idea who did this?"

"Yeah, I have a pretty good idea, but I can't prove it," Fernando said. He told Hank about saving Cassie from Ted Fisher and how Fisher's lawyer, a fancy lawyer from L.A., had tried to buy his silence by giving him a lucrative position as head of security on the movie set if he would sign a nondisclosure agreement. Which he wouldn't.

"So you think somebody working for Fisher attacked you," Hank said.

"I do. To warn me not to testify about Fisher's assaulting Cassie. Fisher's already facing a lawsuit by three women accusing him of sexual assault."

"Two women," Hank reminded him. "Anne Lewis is dead."

"Okay, two women," Fernando repeated. "Now let's get the hell out of here. You lead the way."

The young doctor started to say something as they walked by the nurse's station, but they were out the automatic doors before she could finish her sentence.

They sat in Hank's cruiser without talking for a few minutes. Finally Hank asked, "So what do you think? You wanna go back to the Sagebrush and take it easy for a while or what?"

Fernando couldn't help fussing with the bandage on the left side of his head. "What? Yeah, drop me off at the Sagebrush. I need to change out of this bloody shirt and pick up my cell phone. I left it in my room. I was on my way to breakfast when the sonofabitch hit me."

"You got it." Hank said and started the big engine. He drove down the Paseo to the Sagebrush and pulled up in front. Then he turned to Fernando. "Do you need some help?"

Fernando gave him a dirty look.

"Okay, I'll call you if anything pops," Hank said.

Fernando walked unsteadily through the door and down the hallway to his room. He didn't, as a matter of fact, feel all that damned good. His head throbbed, his legs wobbled, and his vision seemed blurry at the edges, whatever that meant.

When he opened the door of his room he saw that Cassie's suitcase was gone. She'd already left for the airport. Too bad he didn't get a chance to say goodbye. He genuinely liked the woman.

First things first. He took off his bloody shirt and tossed it in the trash. Then he washed his face and examined the bandage on the left side of his head. Not much blood showing, which was a good sign. So he removed the bandage and replaced it with a large band aid. Maybe he could buy a hat to wear over the band aid so he didn't look like a damned fool. A western hat like Hank's or maybe even a baseball cap, even though he hated baseball caps, which didn't even give you protection from the sun, so what was the point?

Next he gobbled two more Tylenol from the bottle he kept in his duffel bag. Got to stay on top of the pain. He'd learned that the hard way over the years.

It took him a while to find his cell phone. For some reason he'd placed it on the counter behind the television, probably to hide it from prospective thieves while he went to breakfast.

He found a text message from Cassie when he plugged in the phone. Sent fifteen minutes earlier, it read: "help, strange van driver, opposite direction, Capulin campground sign".

Fernando panicked. He paced around the room trying to clear his head. He remembered that Capulin Campground was a few miles east of Taos on Highway 64 heading toward Cimarron, just beyond the turnoff to Shadow Mountain Road. Not the way to the Albuquerque airport, for sure. If she were in a van with a strange driver going off road, then she must have been abducted. Why else would she ask for help? It sounded like Fisher's work.

He grabbed the holster with his Smith & Wessen. He didn't have time to get help from Hank. He would have to do this by himself.

An adrenaline rush made him forget his headache and carried him outside the Sagebrush and into his Cherokee. He squinted to minimize his blurred vision as he sped out onto the main drag and then turned right on Paseo del Cañon, which circled the eastern edge of Taos and connected with Highway 64 East. His mind raced as he drove through the outskirts of the city and into the foothills of the Carson National Forest. Minutes later he saw Shadow Mountain Road off to his left and, just beyond, the sign for Capulin Campground.

Fernando pulled off the highway onto a dirt road. He saw the campground through the trees, heavily forested with juniper and ponderosa pine. The road branched off in a semicircle through the trees with campsites on either side of the road. Ahead a green and white tent flapped in the mountain wind. An aging VW Vanagon was parked off to the side, while two old hippies, man and woman, tended an open fire in their metal fire pit. They waved as he drove by. He waved back.

Fernando slowed to a crawl as he entered the heaviest part of the forest. Through the trees he caught a glimpse of a white van in a campsite up ahead. He didn't see the logo of the Sagebrush Airport Shuttle on the van, which didn't surprise him. He figured the van was probably a rental from the movie set. As he drove closer he spotted two people at the campsite. The nearest was a heavy-set man wearing a leather jacket and a baseball cap. He was talking and motioning with his hands. The second was a young woman wearing a familiar navy blue suit sitting on top of a picnic table. Cassie. She sat bent over with her head in her hands.

Fernando didn't waste any time. He parked the Cherokee at the entrance to the campsite, blocking the exit. He jumped out and slammed the door behind him harder than he intended. He no longer felt the pain in his head, only a blind rage fueled by anger and adrenaline.

The heavy-set man spun around and looked at him. "You!"

Cassie raised her head, a good sign.

"Leave her alone," Fernando said, taking his Smith & Wessen out of its holster. He walked quickly across the campsite, the pine needles crunching under his feet.

"Whoa! Take it easy," fat man said and raised his hands. "We're just having a friendly chat. I'm taking her to the airport in Albuquerque."

"You're going the wrong way, pal."

Fat man shrugged. "We're taking I-25. It's faster."

Cassie shook her head angrily. "No! He's trying to intimidate me... keep me from testifying against Ted."

"Did he hurt you?" Fernando asked.

"No, he hasn't gotten that far," she said.

Fernando walked up to fat man and pointed the barrel of the Smith & Wessen at the center of his forehead. "You come near her again and I'll put a bullet right here, you understand?"

Suddenly fat man lunged at the pistol. He was too slow.

Fernando knocked the man's hand away with his left arm, pulled back his right arm, and smashed the pistol across the man's face as hard as he could.

Fat man fell to his knees with both hands on his bloodied face, moaning.

Cassie ran behind Fernando for shelter.

"Now we're even," Fernando said.

Fat man sputtered and cursed on the ground, taking a handkerchief out of his pocket to stop his nosebleed.

Fernando turned to Cassie. "Let's get your suitcase out of the van. I'll take you back to the Sagebrush shuttle."

Cassie followed him to the white van.

"Who is this guy anyway?" Fernando asked, as he opened the back hatch of the van and grabbed her suitcase.

"He's Ted Fisher's bodyguard and driver, Joe Monroe," Cassie said. "He showed up this morning and said he'd give me a lift to the airport. I should have known better."

Fernando deposited the suitcase in the back of the Cherokee. As they drove off fat man was sitting up against the picnic table with a handkerchief over his nose. He didn't wave.

8

After putting Cassie on the Sagebrush Airport Shuttle and saying goodbye for a second time, Fernando walked directly to his room. He needed to pack his belongings and get out of the Sagebrush fast. Ted Fisher and his thug Joe Monroe would be coming for him sooner or later. Probably sooner. He didn't want to be here when they arrived. Best to play it safe and check into someplace out of the way, someplace Hollywood types like Fisher and his lawyer would never imagine staying. He knew just the place: the El Pueblo Lodge, where he usually stayed when he came to Taos. He had a love/hate relationship with the El Pueblo.

Fernando stuffed everything into his duffel bag and left the key cards on the bureau. Then he walked down the hallway to the front desk and checked out, paying with a credit card. He left through a side door and hurried across the parking lot to his Cherokee. As far as he could tell the coast was clear, so he turned onto the Paseo and drove into Taos. Every few blocks he glanced into his rear view mirror to make sure no one was on his tail. Just past Michael's Kitchen he turned left into the funky El Pueblo Lodge, a nineteen sixties style motor lodge with parking in front of every room and a metal chair outside every door. He pulled up in front of the office and waited a few seconds to make sure no one was following. When he was satisfied, he walked into the tiny office.

"Hi--I remember you," the young woman behind the counter said. She wore red-tinted glasses and had raven black hair down to her shoulders. Sorry to say, he didn't remember her.

"Yeah, I'm back," Fernando said. "I'd like the room at the end, where I always stay."

"Okay, you got it," she said. "By the way, why do you always ask for that particular room? No one else seems to want it, maybe because it's off in the trees there, sort of."

"Fewer people to worry about."

She laughed. "O-kay. You want the weekly rate again?"

"No, just one or two nights. I hope."

He signed the form and gave her a credit card imprint.

"You're all set," she said, and handed him two keycards.

Fernando started out the door and then stopped and turned around. "Oh, if anybody comes by asking about me, tell them you haven't seen me. And then let me know right away, okay?"

Perplexed, she asked, "Who would be looking for you? Your wife?"

Fernando laughed at the implication of her question. "No, I'm alone. Not having an affair. I just don't want any visitors."

She nodded, suspicious. "Sure. Whatever you want."

He parked the Cherokee in front of his end room and walked inside. He found the same beat-up furniture, sagging beds and worn easy chair that he remembered from his last visits. The familiarity pleased him. Home sweet home.

He tossed his duffel on the bed and went into the bathroom to take a look at the band aid covering the lump on the side of his head. The lump made his head look lopsided. Like he had a horn or something equally appalling under the band aid. Pissed, he tore off the large band aid and tossed it in the wastebasket. Instead, he took a smaller band aid out of his shaving kit and applied it to the affected area. Problem was the hair prevented the smaller band aid from sticking, so he tore off that too and tossed it in the wastebasket. To hell with it. He was too old to care how he looked.

First things first. He took a seat at the beat-up desk and called Hank on his cell phone.

"Mathews here," Hank answered. "Fernando?"

"Yeah, I wanted to let you know I checked out of the Sagebrush," Fernando said. "Turns out the guy who attacked me does work for Fisher. His name's Joe Monroe and he's Fisher's bodyguard and driver, or so I'm told. He attempted to abduct Cassie this afternoon. I gave him a taste of his own medicine and put Cassie on the Sagebrush Airport Shuttle a few minutes ago. Then I moved to the El Pueblo. Just in case Fisher and his boy come looking for me, which I suspect they will."

"Well, shit, good idea," Hank said. "So you're sure this yahoo's working for Fisher?"

"Absolutely," Fernando said. "Fisher tried real hard to discourage Cassie from testifying against him for attacking her at the Sagebrush."

"The reason I ask is that we got the results of Fisher's DNA test. It didn't match the second condom or any DNA we've found in the room. Cowboy Jack is the only match we have so far."

"Well, keep trying," Fernando said. "Maybe on the body?"

Hank clucked his tongue. "That's tough, what with the body soaking in chlorinated water all night, but I'll ask. I'm just about finished at the office. You want to meet at Michael's Kitchen, say six o'clock?"

"Sounds good, but in the meantime I want to stake out the Taos Inn," Fernando said. "If Fisher arrives with Monroe, I'll give you a call. We need to have another talk with Fisher."

"Just give me a ring, I'll be there."

Fernando left as soon as he put away his cell phone. He put the 'Do Not Disturb' sign on the door to keep housekeeping from meddling with his room. He looked around to make sure the coast was clear and then climbed into his Cherokee. Once on the Paseo he drove down to Bent Street, catty-corner from the Taos Inn. He made a U-turn at the end of Bent Street and came back to the Paseo, parking a few feet from the stop sign. From there he had a clear view of the Taos Inn, both its entrance and its front patio. Then he waited.

A few minutes before six he saw them. Ted Fisher and his hit man, Joe Monroe. They came walking up the sidewalk from the Plaza and went into the Taos Inn patio. They made their way to a patio table off to the side and ordered drinks. Monroe looked like he'd just come from an emergency room or acute care facility. He had a bandage on his right cheek and another triangular-shaped bandage covering his nose. Both eyes looked red and swollen, even from across the street where Fernando was watching with his binoculars.

He called Hank and said, "Let's roll. They just arrived."

"I'm on my way," Hank said.

Fernando waited, watching the two men talk while they sipped their drinks. Minutes later Hank's cruiser appeared on the Paseo. It swerved into Bent Street, did a U-turn in the middle of the street and then parked behind the Cherokee.

Fernando climbed out of the Cherokee and waited for Hank at the stop sign on the corner of Bent and Paseo.

Hank didn't say a word to Fernando or pause to look for traffic. He simply stepped out in the middle of the Paseo and raised his hands high. Traffic slowed to a stop in both directions. Brakes squealed, horns honked. Hank had the attention of everyone on the street, including Fisher and Monroe, both of whom watched wide-eyed from their table.

Fernando followed Hank across the street and into the patio, which was empty except for Fisher and Monroe.

Hank strolled up to their table and said in his best drawl, "Well, well, lookee here, if it ain't Mister Ted Fisher and his stooge."

Fisher had a pained, embarrassed look on his chubby face. He looked around, as though cornered and searching for a way out. "This is Joe Monroe, my driver," he said finally.

"We know who your boy is," Hank shot back.

Monroe started to get up but Hank's big hand on his shoulder discouraged him. "Whoa there, son. I got a message for you and your boss. Either of you lay a hand on another woman in this town and I'll put you in the jail or the hospital, and I don't much care which. You two jackasses understand what I'm telling you? Because I'm not going to say it again."

"Ouch! Fuck!" Moore said when Hank squeezed his shoulder tight. "I understand."

Hank turned to Fisher. "What about you, pretty boy? Do you understand? They might take you to court for this kind of crap in L.A., but around here we have a different way of handling people like you."

Fisher opened his mouth as if to speak but nothing came out. He was flabbergasted that someone would talk to him in that manner.

Hank pointed to Fernando. "My friend here is a former homicide detective from Santa Fe. You're damn lucky he didn't shoot both of you. He still might, you give him another chance."

Hank stared them down, one at a time. Then he grabbed Monroe's arm again. "Now, here's what's gonna happen. You're gonna come into the station for a DNA test tomorrow morning, just like pretty boy here did. If you don't show up, I'll come after you and bring you in one way or another, I don't care which. You understand?"

Monroe nodded.

"And you," Hank said, turning to Fisher. "Don't make me come back again. Next time I won't play nice."

With that, Hank turned and walked out of the patio.

Fernando followed, smiling at the thought that this was Hank playing nice.

9

Fernando awoke with a stiff back. It took him a moment to remember where he was: the El Pueblo Lodge. Unfortunately. He climbed out of bed and stretched, trying to loosen his back muscles. He felt off his game this morning. He really wanted to get back to Santa Fe. He longed for his familiar routine of reading his morning paper and then going down to his office on Canyon Road, but he also felt an obligation to help Hank, who was seriously short-handed. Problem was, they had just about exhausted all leads in the Anne Lewis homicide. He planned to interview Trevor Bowen today, their last hope for a break in the case. That seemed like a remote possibility, given that no one they'd interviewed so far connected Bowen to Anne Lewis.

Once fully awake, he cleaned up as best he could and left a message on Estelle's cell phone. He decided to skip Michael's Kitchen this morning and instead walk down to the Starbucks on the Plaza. Something different. Plus he needed strong coffee this morning, stronger than he could get at Michael's. So he walked down to the Starbucks and bought a large cup of the strongest coffee they had as well as a couple of pastries. The sugar rush gave him some needed energy, so he bought another large cup of coffee and went outside into the Plaza. Just beyond the bandstand he found a sunny bench, so he sat in the sun sipping his coffee and thinking about how to extricate himself from Taos without offending Hank. Not going to be easy. He decided to do the interview with Trevor Bowen and then tell Hank they were at a dead end.

With that in mind, Fernando waited until half past nine to walk down to Ledoux Street, where the movie crew was still shooting. By this time the movie trailers and crew had already arrived. By chance he saw Bonnie Alvarez crossing the Camino de la Placita to Ledoux Street and hurried to catch her. "Bonnie!" he shouted at the woman with short blue hair.

Bonnie turned around and waited for him at the mouth of Ledoux Street. She was in grunge mode today, with cut-off shorts and a Hard Rock T-shirt.

"Where can I find Trevor?" he asked.

"He's down by the Harwood Museum," she said. "Trying to learn his lines. He's not the sharpest tool in the shed. But he is a tool."

Fernando laughed. "Thanks."

He continued on down Ledoux Street, walking past a row of trailers and a group of extras, local actors hired for the crowd scenes. The extras were getting instructions from one of the director's assistants. Up ahead he saw Trevor sitting on a bench in the courtyard out front of the Harwood. Dressed in a bulky commando uniform that made him look like a bloated insect, the actor held a loosely bound script in his lap and appeared to be studying the lines. Bowen read a few lines and then looked up at the sky, repeating the process over and over.

"Howdy," Fernando said.

Trevor looked up and cocked his head, apparently having trouble hearing because of the pointed plastic space helmet on his head, or whatever the hell it was supposed to be.

"Fernando Lopez...we met the other day. I'm helping with the investigation of Anne Lewis' death. I'd like to ask you a couple of questions."

"What?" Trevor asked. Finally he removed his space helmet. "Much better. Anne Lewis, you said?"

Fernando nodded, trying not to laugh. Trevor was wearing so much make-up that his face looked like it had been bronzed. "Right. We understand you may have had a relationship with Anne."

Trevor looked puzzled. "Relationship? You mean a hookup? Sure, we hooked up a few years back when I was making the Marvel movie. She didn't show much interest. I mean, she was cold, man. Cold as ice."

"Did you see her the night she was murdered?" Fernando asked. "In the Sagebrush Cantina--or later in her room?"

"Nope. I stayed clear of Anne. We didn't like each other much. I didn't even go to the Cantina that night. Me and my bros, Tommy and Nicky and Chuck, we went over to Graham's Grill and scouted out the action there. Better looking women, if you know what I mean," Trevor said, winking at Fernando.

"What about later, when you returned to the Sagebrush? Did you see Anne then? In her room?"

Trevor laughed. "No way, man. We ran into some hippie chicks over at Graham's. They were hot. No inhibitions, man. We didn't get back to the Sagebrush until sometime between two and three a.m."

Fernando frowned. Another dead end.

"Sorry, bro, I need to learn these lines or José'll scream at me again. I'm in the doghouse already, man."

Fernando thanked him and walked slowly back to the Plaza. He was tempted to stop by Starbucks for another cup of coffee but decided against it and continued on to El Pueblo. By this time of the morning most of the guests had already checked out, leaving the parking lot nearly deserted. He sat on the metal chair outside his room and considered his options. It seemed foolish to stay in Taos another night, since they had exhausted all leads in the Anne Lewis murder investigation. Better to return to Santa Fe. If something did turn up, he could make it back to Taos in an hour tops.

Having made a decision, Fernando climbed into his Cherokee and followed the Paseo out to the sheriff's office on Lovato Place. Sally rolled her eyes and motioned toward Hank's office as he walked through the front door. What now? Something told him he was better off not knowing.

Hank stood behind his desk, cell phone in hand. He paced slowly from one side of the office to the other. He seemed to be trying to console whoever was on the other end of the conversation.

Fernando waited in the hallway, not eager to get involved in whatever business Hank was discussing. He'd come to tell Hank he intended to head back to Santa Fe this afternoon.

When the call ended, Hank noticed Fernando standing in the hallway. He waved for Fernando to come into his office.

Against his better judgment, Fernando opened the door and stepped into the office.

"Well, shit! You'll never believe this," Hank said, shaking his head. He collapsed in his desk chair.

"That bad?"

"Hah! Worse!" Hank said. "That was Rosalia on the phone. Goddamned Cowboy Jack or Donnie--or maybe both of them--shot and killed a bunch of the Lucero's horses. They came over the mountain and shot 'em long range with rifles. Now Armando and Tony have gone up the mountain after the Ryans. Rosalia's hysterical. She's been hearing gunfire from the mountain and doesn't know who's alive or who's dead. Wants me to come out and stop the shooting. Tell me, how the hell am I supposed to do that? How am I supposed to stop them from killing each other?"

Fernando felt a sinking feeling in the pit of his stomach. He would never be able to abandon Hank now, not under these circumstances.

"Huh? How the hell am I supposed to do that?" Hank repeated.

Fernando sighed. He took a deep breath.

"Maybe that's the answer," Hank said. "Just let them shoot each other. The only way we'll get any peace around here."

Again, Fernando said nothing.

"Awww, shit!" Hank got up and kicked his waste basket across the room, its trash exploding into the air and then falling to the floor. He let loose a string of profanity so loud that Sally came running into the room.

"Are you okay?" Sally asked. "Jesus, Mary, and Joseph, calm down. You have high blood pressure, remember?"

Hank grumbled something and then turned to Fernando. "What do you say? Can I count on you?"

Fernando shook his head in disgust. "Well, I can't let you go up there alone, can I?"

"Good man," Hank said. "Just a minute." He disappeared down the hallway and returned a few minutes later with two Remington 700 rifles. He tossed one to Fernando and stuffed two boxes of ammo in his duty belt.

"You think we'll need sniper rifles?" Fernando asked.

"Who knows? We're going up a mountain," Hank said. He looked around the office quickly and then grabbed his black Stetson. "Let's go."

On the way out Hank turned to Sally. "Tell Roy where we went. Just in case."

"In case of what?" Sally asked.

"Just in case."

10

Hank raced around the Paseo, honking and passing every vehicle that got in his way. Ignoring Fernando, he gripped the steering wheel tightly and drove like a man possessed. He shot up Highway 522 to Questa in less than fifteen minutes. Only Cabresto Canyon Road slowed him down. Neither of them said a single word on the way to the Lucero Ranch.

Hank turned right at the T and bounced up the road past the cornfield to the Lucero Ranch. He pulled into a parking area near the house and set the brake. Rosalia stood on the front porch seemingly talking to the screen door. Only when they climbed out of the cruiser did they notice the mother, Isabel, on the other side of the screen. Her ghostly black shape disappeared into the interior of the house as soon as she saw Hank and Fernando approaching.

Rosalia yelled something and then ran down the porch steps waving a cell phone. "They lost reception up on the mountain--I don't know if Armando and Tony are dead or alive," she wailed.

Hank grabbed Rosalia by her shoulders and held her for a moment. "Okay, Calm down. Tell us what happened."

"Like I told you, the Ryans came over the mountain and started shooting our horses," Rosalia said, trying to catch her breath. "By the time Armando got his gun and started shooting back, they'd killed eight of our horses. I tried to stop Armando from going after them, but he went anyway. And he took Tony with him."

Fernando stepped forward. "Are they on foot?"

Rosalia nodded.

"How long has it been since you heard from your brothers?" Fernando asked.

"About half an hour," she said. "Right before I called you."

"Were either of them injured?"

She shook her head. "I don't think so, but I could hear shooting in the background."

Fernando turned to Hank. "What do you think?"

"Well, I for damn sure can't make it up that mountain on foot, so is there a road or some way to get up there without walking?"

"There's an old forest road that goes almost to the top. It's at the bottom of the hill right before our driveway. Off to the right."

"How rough is the road? Can our cruiser make it up?" Hank asked.

Rosalia glanced at the cruiser. "Maybe. I don't know. I haven't been up there in years."

"What choice do we have?" Fernando asked.

Hank nodded and then took Rosalia back to the house and told her not to worry, that he would check on her brothers. Isabel appeared on the other side of the screen door and stared at Hank.

"Isabel, are you okay?" Hank asked. "Do you need anything?"

The veiled woman, dressed all in black, turned and disappeared into the dark house. A ghost.

Hank returned to the cruiser shaking his head. "She hasn't spoken since Eloy died."

Fernando shrugged.

Before leaving, they walked to the corral to inspect the carnage. They saw eight dead horses sprawled on the ground, pools of blood and shredded horseflesh soaking into the dry sandy earth. The surviving horses had broken through the wooden fence at the back of the corral. They lingered, four of them, in the foothills overlooking the corral, spooked by the grisly death of so many of their herd. Snorting, pawing the ground, the horses gradually moved further into the pines.

"Hard to believe the crazy bastards would actually do something like this--they love these animals," Hank said, mostly to himself, and then turned and walked back to the cruiser with Fernando following.

Once in the cruiser Hank drove back down the bumpy drive. Just beyond the entrance to the ranch he turned off on an overgrown path that looked like an old animal trail more than a forest road. Weeds scraped the cruiser's undercarriage as it plowed through the thick vegetation. It sounded like they were driving a combine harvesting a field of wheat or corn. Then the bumps started, bouncing the cruiser up and down until Hank slowed to a crawl. The road, so-called, curved up and around the hillside above the Lucero Ranch. Halfway up the mountain they came to a rockslide that had buried the road in a wave of boulders.

"There they are," Hank said, pointing to Armando and Tony. The two brothers crouched behind the wall of boulders. They had climbed the mountain on foot.

CRACK! A gunshot rang out from a ridge up ahead.

Tony fired back with his high-powered rifle. CRACK!

Hank pulled off the road behind an outcropping of rock. He and Fernando jumped out of the cruiser, ducking as they made their way around to the rear of the cruiser. Hank opened the trunk and passed one of the Remington 700s to Fernando. They loaded the rifles and then moved carefully toward the wall of boulders, keeping their eyes focused on the ridge above them. Trying to spot the Ryans.

"My brother's injured," Tony said as they took cover behind the boulders. The younger brother looked worried.

Fernando noticed Armando holding his right side. He moved over to the wounded man and touched his shoulder. "Are you hit?"

"I'm okay," Armando said, struggling to steady his rifle and pull the trigger. He seemed to be shaking.

Fernando cursed. "Let me see."

Armando ignored Fernando. Instead, he managed to get off a shot: CRACK! The bullet pinged harmlessly off the ridge ahead, where Cowboy Jack and Donnie were supposedly hiding.

In response the Ryan brothers let loose a barrage of gunfire that smashed into the wall of rocks and splattered them with fragments of stone.

Fernando hit the dirt a little too hard. He landed on his face and ended up with sand in his mouth. He ran his tongue over his teeth and spat. Then he looked over at Hank, who was wiping blood off his forehead with his sleeve. Hank's face was pockmarked with red splotches.

Hank was furious. "This is crazy. We should let them shoot each other and get it over with."

"We still could," Fernando said.

"Enough! Hank said. The big man raised his rifle and positioned it in a V-shaped niche between two boulders. He waited patiently. When he saw a rifle poke out over the ridge he pulled the trigger.

In response one of the Ryans screamed on the ridge and dropped his rifle, which slid down a stone embankment and landed in the weeds below.

"Good shot," Fernando said. Hank was the best marksman with a pistol he'd ever seen. Back in the days of his youth, Hank's nickname had been Sundance, after the Robert Redford character in the "Butch Cassidy and the Sundance Kid" movie. Old Hank wasn't half bad with a rife either.

"Let's go," Hank said and started up the hill. Fernando followed, his Remington pointed at the ridge. They heard the Ryan brothers arguing and screaming at each other up ahead. One of them was hit. Maybe bad.

"This is Sheriff Hank Mathews here--I want you to stop shooting and come down with your hands up!" Hank bellowed at the ridge. "If you don't, I'm gonna shoot both of you!"

Fernando held back to give Hank cover. No need, because they heard the clopping hooves of horses riding away as they approached the ridge. The Ryan boys had ridden away on horseback.

Hank cursed as he struggled to climb the rocky embankment while favoring his arthritic knee. When he reached the base of the sandstone outcropping, he stopped for a moment to massage and flex his knee. Meanwhile, Fernando walked around the sandstone slab, shaped like a hoodoo, and found footprints and drops of blood in the sand where the Ryans had stood moments ago.

"Yeah, there's blood up here," Fernando said. "Not a lot, but it's more than just a flesh wound."

"Anything else?"

Fernando searched the area behind the rock but found nothing of interest. "Nothing but some horseshit over in the trees."

Hank laughed and started back down the embankment to look for the rifle dropped by one of the Ryan brothers. He stumbled and nearly lost his balance as he waded through weeds below the ridge.

"There it is," Hank said, pawing through a patch of snake grass. "Looks like an old single action thirty ought six."

Hank paused to take a glove out of his rear pocket. He put the glove on his left hand. Then he picked up the rifle with his gloved hand and inspected it, finding streaks of blood on the stock. He held the rife out in front of him and carefully carried it back to the cruiser for evidence. He wrapped the rifle in a sheet of plastic and put it in the trunk of the cruiser. He placed his Remington 700 alongside the plastic. Fernando did the same with his Remington.

Leaving Hank, Fernando walked back to the wall of rocks to check on Armando. He found Armando hunched over his rifle, face down. Tony stood off to the side looking petrified.

"What's wrong?" Fernando said.

Tony shook his head. Tears ran down his face.

Fernando rushed to help Armando. He grabbed the older Lucero by his shoulders and turned him over. As he did he saw the pool of thick red blood on the ground and the gaping wound in Armando's abdomen. Tony began to wail as Fernando tried and failed to find a pulse. Desperate now, Fernando fell to his knees and began compressing Armando's chest, pumping with both hands gently at first and then harder when he saw the compression wasn't having any effect.

Just then Hank came hobbling up to the rocks. "Armando? Oh, Christ, don't tell me."

Fernando nodded.

"Help him! You gotta help him!" Tony shouted, getting hysterical.

"Stay calm, Tony," Fernando said, leaving Armando's side. He took the kid aside and comforted him as best he could. Tony put his arms around Fernando and bawled like a baby.

Meanwhile, Hank called for the medevac at Holy Cross Hospital. It wasn't a rescue call.

While they waited for the medevac, Tony sat quietly weeping on a ledge of rock. He would not be comforted, blaming the Ryans for killing his brother and father. Fernando and Hank walked out on a small meadow down the road a ways, the flattest area within eyesight. Thirty minutes later they heard the copter approaching. Hank raised his hands and waved at the pilot, who dipped his blades to acknowledge contact. After circling twice, the copter descended slowly, kicking up dust and dead brush as it set down on the dry, dusty meadow.

Out of the copter jumped a young medic wearing green scrubs. He ducked below the copter's blades before the pilot cut the engine and ran across the meadow to where Hank and Fernando were waiting.

"What's the situation?" the medic asked.

Fernando shook his head. "He's over by the rocks. I couldn't find a pulse."

Behind them Tony continued to weep, but quieter now. He turned away to hide his tears.

The medic ran to the rock wall and set down his bag. He knelt over Armando and began searching for a pulse. When he saw the wound and the pool of blood he stopped. He examined Armando's eyes and then waved at the pilot to bring a stretcher.

An older man with a neatly trimmed beard stepped out of the helicopter and unloaded a stretcher. At first he moved with a sense of urgency but then, when he saw his co-worker standing up, slowed down to a leisurely walk. As if they communicated without speaking.

The older medic knelt beside Armando and conducted a quick examination. The two medics exchanged a few words, talking in hushed tones so that Tony couldn't hear. When they finished, the two of them loaded Armando on the stretcher and carried him to the copter. While the other medic started the engine, the younger one came back to the wall of rocks. "One of you will need to come with us to provide information," he said. "We'll be at Holy Cross."

Both Fernando and Hank looked at Tony.

“I’m his brother,” Tony said, standing up and drying his eyes. “I’ll go with you.”

Tony grabbed his rifle and started to follow the medic.

“Wait a minute, the gun stays with me,” Hank said. With that, Hank reached out and yanked the rifle out of Tony’s hands.

Tony started to say something but then thought better about it and nodded. Then he followed the medic to the copter and climbed aboard.

Fernando and Hank watched the big bird lift off. It circled once and then headed southeast toward Holy Cross Hospital in Taos.

Shaking his head, Hank walked back to the cruiser. He wrapped Tony’s rifle in plastic and then laid it in the trunk with the others. Then he slammed the trunk closed. Hard.

Hank turned to Fernando. “Now we gotta tell Isabel and Rosalia.”

“You have to tell them,” Fernando said.

Hank frowned. “Lucky me.”

11

Rosalia sat on the porch waiting for them as they drove into the Lucero Ranch. She shot up from her bench as soon as she saw them. She started down off the porch and then stopped, as if afraid to hear whatever news they were bringing her.

Hank parked off to the side of the house and climbed out of the cruiser. He hung his head and walked slowly to the porch. Fernando stayed back, letting Hank do the talking.

Rosalia knew at first glance that something had gone terribly wrong up on the mountain. Not a word had been said, but she burst into tears and ran over to Hank, who wrapped his arms around her like a big bear and held her while she wept.

"I'm so sorry, Rosy, Armando was already gone when we got there," Hank said, stretching the truth a bit. "There was nothing we could do to save him. Tony went with him on a medevac to Holy Cross Hospital. You or your mom will have to go down to help him with the paper work and give him a ride home."

"Those stinking Ryans murdered him!" she wailed.

"I reckon so," Hank said. "We winged one of them, trying to protect Tony. We'll be paying them a visit as soon as we leave here."

Rosalia sobbed quietly on Hank's shoulder. "It's you men. What's wrong with you? Why do you have to be so violent? I tried to talk to Armando, but he would never listen. He just wanted revenge. First Jack Ryan and then Morris. On our side daddy and now Armando. Where does it stop? How many more will have to die?"

Hank sighed. "I don't know, darlin'. I just don't know. Sometimes I think human nature's to blame. Men especially. They seem programmed to fight and kill."

While Hank comforted Rosalia, Fernando noticed her mother, Isabel, standing inside the screen door watching them. A black veil over her face hid her emotions.

As soon as Fernando moved toward the porch Isabel disappeared into the dark interior of the house. Again.

Fernando climbed the steps to the porch and stood outside the screen door. "Mrs. Lucero? Can we talk?" he asked.

"No, the devil's outside," she said. "I can't come out!"

Fernando heard a door slam inside the dark house. He gave up and rejoined the others.

Hank patted Rosalia on the back and then released her. "You'll need to comfort your mama," he said. "Can you drive her to the hospital, or do you want me to take the both of you?"

"Mama won't come," she said. "I'll have to go by myself. I need to bring Tony home anyway."

Hank took out his pocket notebook and wrote down directions to Holy Cross Hospital and some telephone numbers for Rosalia. "If you need any help, just give me a call, okay?"

She nodded, drying her eyes.

"Anything you need, I'm serious," Hank said. Then he turned and walked to the cruiser, where Fernando was waiting for him.

On their way out of the ranch Fernando told Hank about his brief conversation with Isabel. "She said she couldn't come outside to talk with me because the devil was outside."

"Ain't that the truth," Hank said.

When they turned into the Ryan's driveway, they again found the iron gate closed and locked with a chain and padlock. Hank uttered a string of profanity as they slowed to a stop. He parked in front of the gate and crawled out of the cruiser. He walked around to the rear of the car and opened the trunk, taking out a heavy duty chain cutter. "Look what I brought from my tool shed? I'm tired of fucking around with these people. Enough's enough!"

With that, Hank walked to the gate and grabbed the chain that secured the gate with his big cutters. He grunted and wrested with the massive cutters until the chain snapped. Then he pulled the chain off the gate and tossed it into the ditch. The padlock followed.

Fernando jumped out of the cruiser and opened the gate wide as Hank drove through. Then he climbed back into the shotgun seat.

"Let me do the talking," Hank said as he drove up the lane toward Donnie's barricade. "This is a delicate situation. I'll have to find a way to get through to them. All this horseshit about an eye for an eye. They started the feud and they have to end it. Whether they like it or not."

Donnie was nowhere to be seen, which was not surprising. Most likely he was still up on the mountain with Cowboy Jack.

Hank parked alongside Cowboy Jack's black Dodge Ram pickup, halfway between the ranch house and the barn. No one appeared to be home, but Hank walked to the front door of the house and knocked anyway. Instantly the door opened a crack. Someone must have heard them drive into the yard. That someone was standing just inside the door. Hank stood back from the door and reached for his Colt .45, not taking any chances.

"Ruth? Is that you?" Hank asked.

"What do you want?" Ruth asked from behind the door.

"Open the door, I need to talk to you," Hank said, anger in his voice.

The chain lock rattled and the door opened. Ruth stood inside the door, holding a Glock pistol pointed directly at them.

Hank raised his hands, still holding his Colt. "Damnit, Ruth, put the gun away, there's been too much killing already today."

"Yeah? Like who?"

"Armando Lucero, that's who," Hank said. "I reckon your boys shot and killed him up on the mountain."

"He deserved it!" she snapped. "He killed Morris, my oldest. They owed us a brother. Now we're even."

"Hell of a way to look at it, Ruth. The killing's got to stop. Where's Jack Junior and Donnie now?"

"I don't know. They haven't come back," she said. "What're you going do to them, anyway?"

Hank frowned. "Well, for starters, I'm going to ask them some questions, and then I just might arrest whichever one shot Armando."

"Why didn't you arrest Armando for shooting Morris?" Ruth replied.

"Because I didn't see Armando shoot Morris," Hank said. "I did see your boys shoot Armando."

Ruth returned the Glock to her shoulder holster. "Yeah, well good luck finding them. They took their camping gear when they left this morning. They should be all the way to Latir peak by now."

With that, Ruth turned and walked into the house, leaving them standing on the porch.

Hank called after her. "Ruth, listen to me. You Ryans started this feud and you Ryans have to end it. Do you hear me?"

Ruth slammed the door closed behind her.

Fernando looked at Hank. "What now?"

Hank ignored the question, giving Fernando a dirty look instead. He climbed into the cruiser and gunned the big engine. He waited for Fernando to get in and then took off in a cloud of dust. "I'm for damn sure not gonna chase them boys up Latir Peak. That's near thirteen thousand feet."

"I don't think you have to worry," Fernando said. "Chances are

Cowboy Jack and Donnie are hiding in the barn or somewhere else on the ranch."

Hank gave him a confused look. "What do you mean?"

"Didn't you see the corral? Cowboy Jack's horse was there, still sweating from the ride back from the shootout on the mountain. Looked like his saddle had been taken off not long ago."

"You wanna go back?" Hank asked, taking his foot off the gas pedal.

"No, I think it'll be easier to grab him in town," Fernando said. "Cowboy Jack is a player. He shows up at the Sagebrush Cantina every night hoping to score. He likes to bed out-of-town women who are passing through. Professional women, sexually liberated women. Like Anne Lewis and Bonnie Alvarez and who knows how many others from the movie set. All we have to do is stake out the Cantina and wait. We'll get our chance. Probably sooner than later."

Hank thought about that for several moments. "Well, hell, I don't know, maybe you're right."

"Thing is, you'll have to decide what to do when we get him," Fernando said. "Whether to arrest him--or just take him in for questioning. Try to scare him into behaving."

Hank pondered the question as they drove down Highway 522 toward Taos, with the sun beginning to set in the southwest, the sky streaked with crimson. The end of another frustrating day. Who knew what the night would bring.

"One thing's for sure, hanging out at the Sagebrush sure beats climbing Latir Peak," Hank said. "Hell, that's more'n thirteen thousand feet, now that I think about it."

"The beer's colder, anyway," Fernando added.

12

They made a plan over dinner at Michael's Kitchen. Fernando would stake out the Sagebrush Cantina beginning about seven in the evening when the music got started. Hank would remain at his office, a few blocks away. Fernando would call Hank the moment he spotted Cowboy Jack and the two of them would confront the young man. If Cowboy Jack refused to answer questions, then they would bring him in and book him on suspicion of murder, even if they would have to release him next morning for lack of evidence. Processing the physical evidence, mainly Cowboy Jack's rifle, would take time and involve working with forensics on fingerprints and DNA, not to mention ballistics, which would take longer. A long night in the slammer was the best they could do under the circumstances.

Fernando arrived at the Sagebrush shortly after the music started. A few people were already dancing on the wooden floor as he walked through the door into the dark Cantina. He saw the movie crowd gathered up front around the bar. He recognized Bonnie and the two leads, Trevor and Jacqueline at different ends of the bar. Even the director José Sousa stood at the far end of the bar talking to an older man with snow-white hair wearing a suit who he recognized as Gary Clark, the hotel manager, who he'd met earlier. Next to Clark stood none other than Joe Monroe with the triangular bandage still on his nose.

That pissed him off. Monroe was the last person he wanted to see here or anywhere else. The man couldn't take a hint. What did he have to do to get rid of fat man? Shoot him?

When Monroe happened to glance over and see him, Fernando flashed him a big smile. Monroe turned away quickly, a snarl on his face. Apparently the man wasn't giving up. Which meant trouble.

Fernando didn't see Cowboy Jack anywhere in the room. That didn't surprise him at this early hour. The night was young for people looking for hookups. He found a table along the side wall, near the entrance to the old part of the hotel, now closed to guests except for the restrooms. From here he had a clear view of the bar and the dance floor. When the waitress appeared, sashaying across the floor to the beat of the music, he ordered his usual Modelo draft.

"You want fresh lime with that?" she asked, a buxom blonde with her hair woven into green tinted braids.

"No, ma'am, just the beer," he said, watching her walk away in her skin-tight leotards and spandex top.

By the time he finished his Modelo the room had filled with party animals, dancing and drinking and talking all at once. The music got louder and faster as the evening wore on. The dancers whirled nonstop around the dance floor. Everyone had their party on tonight, except Fernando and Monroe, who kept watching each other from across the Cantina. Eventually people began to gather around the dance floor to watch the dancers, blocking his view of the bar. He couldn't see a damn thing. He had to stand up every so often to see if Cowboy Jack had arrived.

Halfway through his second Modelo Fernando had to push a couple of guys out of his line of vision. That's when he saw Cowboy Jack. The cocky young man stood at the bar in his white western hat, his right hand bandaged from Hank's shot back on the mountain. Next to him stood another even younger man who looked like a teenager, a familiar teenager. Fernando realized the teenager was Donnie, Cowboy Jack's younger brother. That puzzled him, because Donnie wasn't old enough to drink legally in the state of New Mexico. So why bring him?

Fernando waited a few minutes and then walked out of the Cantina with his head lowered trying not to be noticed. Outside the cool mountain air invigorated him. He was relieved to get away from the noise and the stench of too much human flesh crammed into such a small space.

He walked under a massive portico that marked the Sagebrush's original entrance. Like most everything in the original building, it was no longer used. He found a spot in the shadows and called Hank on his cell phone.

"Cowboy Jack's here," Fernando said when Hank answered.

"I'm on my way," Hank replied.

Fernando moved out of the shadows and into the parking lot. He wanted to meet up with Hank so they could work together. He'd let Hank take the front door and he would come in through the patio in back.

Halfway to his Cherokee he heard a voice behind him. His spirits sank.

"Not so fast. You can run, but you can't hide."

Fernando spun around to see Joe Monroe step out of the shadows. Monroe held something in his hand. Light from a three-quarter moon glinted off what appeared to be a pistol.

"What do you want, Monroe?"

"You! I want you!" Monroe said. "Now put your gun on the ground."

Fernando laughed. "You're gonna shoot me out here, with a hundred people inside that door?"

"That's up to you, Lopez. Put your gun on the ground and raise your hands or you'll find out."

Fernando held out his right hand and then moved the hand in slow motion toward the open carry holster on his belt. Easy peasy.

Just then Hank's cruiser pulled into the parking lot behind Fernando. The cruiser's headlights splashed Monroe, momentarily blinding him. Monroe fired wildly. The bullet ricocheted off the pavement.

Fernando jumped behind the nearest vehicle, a gigantic Toyota Land Cruiser. He pulled out his Smith & Wessen and listened. He heard nothing. When he glanced around the Land Cruiser he didn't see Monroe. Either the man had run off quietly or vanished into thin air.

"What the hell's going on?" Hank shouted from the parking lot. "Who's shooting?"

"Joe Monroe took a shot at me," Fernando shouted back. "He seems to have disappeared."

Hank stepped forward out of the shadows and looked around. Satisfied, he hurried across the open parking lot to where Fernando waited. "What? Are Monroe and Cowboy Jack in cahoots?"

"Not as far as I know," Fernando said.

While they talked a small crowd of onlookers gathered outside the Cantina. Some of the partygoers still carried drinks in their hands. Having heard the gunshot, they had come out for the spectator sport.

"Anybody hurt?" the bartender shouted from the door of the Cantina.

"Anybody dead?" some wise guy hollered.

Fernando waved them off. "Go back inside and enjoy yourselves. There's nothing to see out here."

He waited until the crowd went back into the Cantina and then followed a sidewalk around behind the main building, where Monroe may have vanished. Hank brought up the rear, Colt .45 in hand.

Behind the building they came to an outdoor patio protected by a curving adobe wall. Straight ahead they saw a walkway through an arched adobe gate into an enclosed courtyard. Fernando led the way, moving quietly to the walkway and peering around the corner of the gate. He saw no one in the semi-dark courtyard, surrounded on all sides by two-story room blocks. The rooms looked ancient. The wooden stairways up to the second-floor rooms looked especially dilapidated, like they would collapse if anyone tried to climb them. Fernando doubted the upper level rooms were still in use, since all of them looked dark. While he scanned the room blocks, a northwesterly wind whistled through the courtyard.

Fernando moved carefully into the courtyard, hearing Hank lumbering behind him. Two large cottonwood trees in the courtyard threw jagged shadows across the grass in the center of the yard. The upper ramparts were lost in darkness. A perfect hiding place for Monroe. Anyone venturing out into the open courtyard would be a sitting duck. The only solution was to separate and go up on the ramparts, where they could use the darkness to their advantage.

Fernando stopped Hank and motioned for him to climb the stairway on the east side of the courtyard. He would take the stairway on the northern side.

Hank nodded and headed for the eastern side.

Fernando crept over to the northern stairway. The rickety wooden steps creaked and groaned as he climbed up one step at a time to the second floor. He paused between steps to make sure the aged wood would hold. The dark brown paint of the stairway and the doors of the rooms above added to the gloom. He could barely see ten feet in front of him. He stopped every few steps to listen. He heard nothing other than the muted pounding of the music coming from the Cantina and the wind howling across the ramparts.

He crept along the corridor to the end of the northern and then the western sides. He saw no sign of Joe Monroe or any human activity until he came to the southern side. Halfway down the corridor he saw a dim light coming from one of the rooms ahead. The light seemed to be moving from one side of the curtained window to the other. He stopped, waiting.

Suddenly the door to the room opened and a tall, dark man stepped into the shadows. Too tall to be Monroe. The man waited for him to approach and then said, "Stay away from room one hundred twelve--there's a ghost in there."

"Yeah?" Fernando asked, looking at the number on the door to the man's room. It read 112.

The stranger watched as Fernando walked by, not speaking.

Fernando glanced into the room as he walked by. The room appeared totally empty. And dark, except for the one dim light coming from somewhere in the interior of the room.

Nearing the end of the southern corridor Fernando looked back but the man had vanished. The door to room 112 was closed.

"Let's get the hell out of here," Fernando said when he met up with Hank. He decided not to tell Hank about the man in room 112.

They walked down the rickety staircase on the southern side of the compound and then around to the front of the Sagebrush. By this time all the gawkers had lost interest and gone back inside the Cantina, leaving the parking lot deserted.

Fernando stopped before opening the door to the Cantina. "I saw Cowboy Jack standing at the bar along the far wall. Let me show you."

"Oh yeah--I plum forgot about Cowboy Jack in all the excitement," Hank said, shaking his head.

Hank followed Fernando through the door.

Inside the music pounded louder than ever. The room seemed to throb as they walked through the throng of dancers on the dance floor.

Fernando pointed to the end of the bar. "There. Cowboy Jack was standing over there talking to someone, a kid who looked even younger than Jack. I think it might have been Donnie."

Hank frowned. "Well, he for damn sure ain't there now. So we're back to square one."

Cowboy Jack had disappeared. Once again.

13

Nightmares kept Fernando tossing and turning most of the night. He dreamed of tip-toeing down a long, dark corridor toward a mysterious room at the very end. A red neon sign above the door blinked on and off: 112, 112. Suddenly the door to the room opened and out stepped a tall man wearing a mask of a human skull. Inside his mask the man's eyes and mouth glowed neon red. The masked man held an old-fashioned long-barrel pistol in his right hand, which he raised slowly to eye level and sighted directly at Fernando. The pistol fired in a burst of white smoke.

The explosion jolted him awake. He fought his way out of the damp bed sheets and sat on the edge of the bed covered in sweat. He checked the time: half past eight, much later than he ordinarily slept. He showered and cleaned up quickly and then walked down to Michael's Kitchen for breakfast. Huevos Rancheros and three cups of coffee revived him enough to face the day, whatever it would bring. He had no idea what Hank had planned for today. At this point he'd given up trying to predict events. They'd been going helter skelter from one crime scene to another and none of them seemed to connect. From the Sagebrush to the mountain to the Sagebrush to the mountain, repeatedly. To what end?

Fernando had no more than stepped outside Michael's Kitchen when his cell phone rang. He sat down on the bench out front and answered the call, seeing Hank's name and number on the screen.

"Hank, what's the plan?" Fernando asked.

"We're getting search and arrest warrants for Cowboy Jack," Hank said. "Should be ready this afternoon. Can you hang tight until then?"

"Sure. What time?"

"I'll get back to you," Hank said and clicked off.

Fernando walked back to the El Pueblo thinking about how to spend the morning while waiting for Hank's call. He didn't have to think long, because his cell phone rang again while walking across the parking lot to his room. This time he didn't recognize the number.

"Mr. Lopez, this is Bonnie Alvarez again...from the movie set," a woman said. "Remember, you told me to call if I had any new information? Well, something else has happened that you should know."

"Sure, thanks for calling," Fernando said, recognizing the voice now.

"It concerns Cowboy Jack again," she said. "Can we meet somewhere downtown? I'd rather tell you in person. We don't start shooting until mid-afternoon today, so I'm free until then."

"Okay, how about the Starbucks for coffee?" Fernando asked.

"Tea for me, but sure, I can be there...say, ten o'clock?"

"I'll be there," Fernando said.

He went for a long walk along Kit Carson Road to kill time, stopping at the Mabel Dodge Luhan House to visit with Francis Rose, a friend who worked at the reception desk. Afterwards he walked downtown and arrived at the Starbucks near the Plaza a few minutes before the arranged hour. It turned out Bonnie had arrived even earlier. He found the young woman with short blue hair sitting a table when he walked into the Starbucks. Wearing jeans and a T-shirt, she waved and sipped her tea. He stood in line to order his coffee with extra cream and sugar and then joined her at the table.

"Thanks for calling," Fernando said. "What's this about Cowboy Jack?"

Bonnie pushed her tea aside. "I told you Jack was something of a ladies man, right? Well, it turns out he spent last night with Kim Edwards, who's a friend of mine. She works as the armorer for the weapons used on the set, mostly by Trevor. She takes care of the guns and blank ammunition and delivers them when needed for a particular scene."

He nodded. "I'm familiar."

"So at breakfast this morning she told me what happened last night. She said during sex Jack had gotten increasingly violent, biting and even choking her. After breakfast she showed me teeth marks on her breasts. She said the bites were so painful she could barely get dressed this morning."

"How did she get away from him?" Fernando asked.

"She didn't," Bonnie said. "As they finished he grabbed her around the neck and choked her. She managed to fight him off by biting his hand. Then, when he released her, he had the nerve to ask if he could bring someone in to join them, just like he's done with me and other hookups. I told you about this, remember?"

Fernando nodded. "You did. A threesome."

Bonnie nodded.

"Does he have a history of being violent with women?" Fernando asked.

"No, not really. Like I said, he's known as something of a ladies man," she said. "I know several women on the set who've slept with him, but this is the first time I've heard of him being violent."

"I can't say I'm surprised, given his situation," Fernando said. "He's a wanted man. He shot and killed a man yesterday."

"He's a murderer?" Bonnie asked, a little too loudly. Everyone in the Starbucks turned to look at her. "Oh, my God," she said, shaking her head.

"You should tell the other women he's been hooking up with to avoid him, if he does come around the Sagebrush," he said.

She nodded. "Of course."

"How can I find Kim Edwards? I'd like to get as much information as I can. She's staying at the Sagebrush, yes?"

Bonnie nodded. "And she'll be at the Mabel Dodge Luhan House later. That's where they're shooting this evening."

"The Luhan House, that's interesting," Fernando said.

"Yeah," Bonnie said, rolling her eyes. "The mob of awakened dead are going to have a shoot-out with the awakened dead of the Luhan House, including Dennis Hopper and some of his wild friends who lived there in the nineteen seventies."

Fernando laughed.

"It's true," Bonnie said. "Today all the scripts are written by twenty-something men--boys, really--who've grown up on video games and Marvel Comics. They live in a video game world."

"I can believe that," Fernando said.

Bonnie fidgeted with her teacup. She glanced at her watch and then at the door. "I just wish they'd finish shooting so we could get the hell out of here! That's all I want. To go home."

"How much more shooting do they have?" he asked.

"A day or two more, if all goes well," she said. "We're supposed to have the final shoot tomorrow back at the graveyard. Some medicine man from Taos Pueblo will recite a magic incantation and Trevor Bowen will appear with bullets filled with a magic herb from Blue Lake. Trevor will distribute the bullets to a posse of Taos citizens who will shoot the awakened dead with the magic bullets. Then all the awakened dead will miraculously climb back in their graves and be dead happily ever after. What a crock of shit!"

Fernando nodded. "I won't argue with that."

Bonnie glanced at her watch again. "I gotta go. I'm all nerves."

"You worried about Jack?"

She nodded. "Last night he came to my door first. I told him I wasn't in the mood, so he went on to Kim's door. What if he comes back tonight? Knowing what I know now, I'm scared to death."

"Do you have any protection?" Fernando asked.

"You mean a gun? No, I don't want anything to do with them."

"Then you might consider rooming with another of the women on the set," Fernando said. "And keep your cell phone nearby at all times in case Cowboy Jack shows up at your door."

Bonnie nodded. "I might ask Kim and maybe Lilly, the costume designer. Lilly has a suite. Maybe the three of us could stay there until the end of the week. Hopefully we'll be finished by then."

"Good idea."

She finished her tea and got up to go.

"You have my card," Fernando said. "Call me if you need help. Any time of day. I'm serious."

Bonnie laughed. "I hope I don't have to do that, but thanks." With that she turned and walked out of the Starbucks.

Fernando took his time finishing his coffee. He had no idea when, or even if, Hank would be able to secure a search warrant for the Ryan Ranch. That left him hanging. What he really wanted to do was go home to Santa Fe, but he felt an obligation to see this through. For Hank.

Leaving Starbucks, he walked up the east side of the Plaza heading north toward the El Pueblo. He noticed a few people on the Plaza, most sitting on benches. It was too early for the afternoon tourist crowd to descend on the downtown area. One person, in particular, seemed to be watching him from a bench near the bandstand. A big man wearing a blue nylon windbreaker and a baseball cap pulled down low on his forehead. It took him a moment to realize the man watching him was Joe Monroe, without the bulbous nose bandage. The sight of Monroe infuriated Fernando. Every time he turned around the guy seemed to reappear.

Fernando made a split decision. He decided to confront Monroe and tell the fat man he had nothing to do with Ted Fisher's lawsuits, so fuck off.

Pivoting, Fernando jaywalked across the street and walked angrily into the Plaza. When Monroe saw him coming, the fat man jumped up and ran off toward the far corner of the Plaza.

Fernando followed at a steady pace. He'd be damned if he'd run after the guy. If Monroe wanted to have it out here and now, then bring it on. The sooner the better. Get it over with.

But Monroe had no such intention. Instead, the fat man took off running and headed north up Teresina Lane, across the public parking lot, and then disappeared on Bent Street.

Fernando stood in the parking lot waiting in case Monroe changed his mind. He didn't.

Ted Fisher needed to call off his boy before someone got hurt.

14

Fernando walked back to the El Pueblo and called the Sagebrush, asking to be connected to Kim Edwards' room. The phone in her room rang and rang until he finally gave up and clicked off. Instead of the Sagebrush, he decided to check out the Mabel Dodge Luhan House to see if the movie crew had begun to set up for their evening shoot. Even though the Luhan House was in easy walking distance, he chose to take the Cherokee in case Hank called and wanted him to come immediately. He drove down to the Plaza and turned left on Kit Carson Road and then, two blocks later, left on Morada Lane.

Once on Morada he saw the movie trailers ahead, some parked along Morada and others in the large parking lot of the Luhan House, which was now a bed and breakfast inn and conference center. The name was a bit deceptive because the property included multiple buildings. The big adobe house, built on a slight rise, overlooked several smaller buildings below, some used for guests and others idle and in a state of disrepair. He turned into the parking area and pulled up near the stairway leading to the courtyard of the big house. Several people from the movie crew were gathered in the courtyard talking. He didn't see the director or any of the actors yet, only members of the crew setting up for the shoot that evening.

Fernando had been at the Luhan House many times over the years, beginning in the 1970s when Dennis Hopper owned the property. He and a couple of his pot-head friends from Santa Fe High would come up on weekends to party with the artists and hippies that hung out with Hopper. Back when he was single, which seemed like a million years ago.

Last year, he'd been hired to find a well-known Santa Fe historian who disappeared while staying at the Luhan House. It turned out that Kate Isaacs had been kidnapped by two psychopathic brothers with the help of one of the groundskeepers who worked at the Luhan House. Unfortunately, the brothers murdered Kate before she could be rescued.

Hank had helped with the search, which is why Fernando felt indebted to him now.

Fernando climbed out of the Cherokee and walked up the stairs into the courtyard. Up close the sprawling century-old adobe house was a sight to behold. The oddly shaped structure contained some two dozen rooms on the first and second levels, none of which were plumb or level. A partial third level, one of Mabel's bedrooms, rose above the rest of the house like a tower, complete with rows of blank windows overlooking the grounds. Vigas, chimneys, and iron weather vanes cluttered the roof creating a bizarre, slightly ominous look. All three levels sagged and jutted out every which way, threatening to collapse in a huge pile of adobe, glass, and timbers.

Fernando had the same reaction every time he saw the house. It looked as if the house had no design but was instead assembled one level and one wing at a time by someone who happened to be mad.

He followed an older, white-hair man carrying a box of sound equipment. They stepped up on a long porch under a veranda. On the side of the Luhan House, near the office, he spotted a tile mosaic of a mounted Don Quixote. The delusional Don Quixote sat on his horse holding a lance, ready to do battle. He hoped the mosaic wasn't an omen, a sign their predicament was as ill-conceived and futile as Don Quixote's.

Fernando stood aside. He waited until the old guy placed the box he was carrying on a bench and then asked where he could find Kim Edwards.

"The armorer? She'd be down in her trailer," he said, pointing to the parking lot. "The one there by the maintenance garage."

"Much obliged," Fernando said. He walked back to the parking lot and then across the gravel to the trailer parked near the garage. He found the door to the trailer open, a good indication that Kim Edwards was inside.

As he approached she stepped out of the trailer and headed for the Luhan House, a tall big-boned woman with spiky brown hair and black bedroom eyes. Another striking woman, L.A. style. Were they all this arresting?

"Kim?" he asked, getting her attention.

She gave him the once over.

"I'm Fernando Lopez, a private investigator working with the Taos County Sheriff," he said. "I wonder if I could ask you a few questions about Jack Ryan Junior, or Cowboy Jack. He's wanted for murder."

At the mention of murder she stopped dead in her tracks. "Cowboy Jack? Really?" she asked. "You mean for the murder of Anne Lewis?"

Fernando shook his head. "No, a man up in Questa named Armando Lucero. But he's also a suspect in the Lewis murder. Bonnie Alvarez said you'd spent time with him last night."

Kim laughed. "Good old Bonnie."

"She said Cowboy Jack was violent and tried to harm you," Fernando said.

Nodding, Kim said, "Yeah, he acted differently last night. I figured something must be wrong."

"What do you mean differently?"

"Well...at first he was the same old Cowboy Jack," she said, pausing to think carefully about what she wanted to say and how she wanted to say it. "He even talked about running away together. Said he'd found an old farmhouse near Arroyo Seco where we could go off grid, just the two of us. I couldn't believe it. I hardly know him, and here he was talking about living together off grid. Talk about weird."

"What was your response?" Fernando asked.

Kim frowned. "I think I offended him. I mean, his proposal was so absurd. I laughed and told him no, I couldn't move to Arroyo Seco. No way. My work was in Los Angeles."

"Did he give you an address...a specific location for this farmhouse in Arroyo Seco?" Fernando asked.

Kim shook her head. "No, but when I turned him down his attitude changed instantly. Like Jekyll and Hyde. He got impatient and wanted to have sex right away. And rough, not like our previous meetings. Like he just wanted to get it over with. Then when he finished he wanted to bring someone else in to join us."

"For a threesome," Fernando said. "Just like he wanted to do with Bonnie Alvarez."

"Exactly. I said no and told him to get the hell out of my room," Kim said. "That's when he grabbed me by the neck and started choking me. I panicked when he wouldn't let go. I really thought he was going to kill me. So I bit his hand and kneed him in the crotch to get him off me, and then I opened the door and screamed for help. When I screamed he grabbed his clothes and ran out the door to the courtyard before anyone arrived. Good riddance."

Fernando took a moment to reflect on what he'd heard. "Did he say anything else about this move to Arroyo Seco?"

"Just that he wanted to get away from his mother's ranch and go off grid with me," Kim said, laughing. "How can you go off grid in Arroyo Seco? It's right next to Taos, yes?"

Fernando shrugged. "Hard to imagine. It's pretty close."

"Hard to imagine anyone wanting to!" she said. "I mean, wake up!

It's the twenty first century the last time I checked! Who wants to go off in the hills and live like a couple of hillbillies?"

"Not someone from Los Angeles," he said.

Kim gave him a funny look.

"So do you want to press charges?"

"No, not really. I just never want to see him again," she said.

Fernando nodded. "Do you have any protection?"

Kim laughed. "I'm an armorer. I specialize in guns. I can take care of myself. If he tries to come in my room again I'll shoot the fucker, okay?"

"Good," Fernando said and then quickly regretted it.

"If you'll excuse me, I need to get to work now," she said and continued on her way to the Luhan House.

Fernando watched her walk across the parking lot. He had no doubt she could take care of herself. He didn't know what to think about Cowboy Jack going off grid in Arroyo Seco. What kind of fantasy was that?

He climbed into his Cherokee and drove back to the El Pueblo. Once there he decided to take a nap. Sometime later a pounding on the door woke him. When he opened the door he found a maid from housekeeping wanting to clean his room. He took the hint and abandoned ship.

Fernando didn't know what the hell to do next. He still hadn't heard from Hank about the warrants. So he walked across the parking lot and sat on a bench in front of the office and called Hank on his cell phone.

"Howdy, Fernando," Hank said. "We're still on a holding pattern over here. We did get the DNA match from Forensics. They found Cowboy Jack's DNA on the condom in Anne Lewis' room. But we're still waiting for the ballistics report."

"Okay."

"Should be sometime this afternoon. Hopefully sooner than later."

"Not to throw a wrench in our plans," Fernando said, "but I just found out Cowboy Jack got violent with another woman at the Sagebrush last night when she refused him. Seems he wanted her to run away with him and go off grid. He said he was moving to an old farmhouse in Arroyo Seco, of all places. She said no thank you and he tried to choke her."

Hank laughed. "No shit? How can Arroyo Seco be off grid? It's only a few miles from Taos?"

"My thoughts exactly."

"Well, hell, then why don't you check out this Arroyo Seco business while Roy and I pay a visit to the Ryan Ranch. That is, as soon as we get the warrants."

"Sounds good. Keep me informed," Fernando said and clicked off.

Now that he didn't have to go up the mountain yet again, Fernando felt liberated. He was damn tired of driving to Questa and damn tired of the Ryans and the Luceros. He filled the Cherokee with gas on the Paseo and then headed out Highway 522 west to the turnoff to Highway 150 north. From there he took Highway 230 into the tiny village of Arroyo Seco, a Sesame Street smorgasbord of brightly colored arts and crafts shops owned by a bunch of old hippies who'd lived there since the Dennis Hopper era of the nineteen seventies. Trimmed in blue, red, and yellow, the adobe and frame buildings were in various stages of disrepair. They included pottery and fine art galleries, restaurants, and a general store.

Fernando drove through the downtown area helter-skelter looking for Cowboy Jack's black Dodge Ram. He followed El Salto Road, the main drag, all the way to the edge of the National Forest. Then he retraced his route by driving up and down the side streets perpendicular to El Salto Road. Nothing. No sign of Cowboy Jack or the black pickup anywhere.

On his way out of town he pulled up in front of Arroyo Seco Mercantile, an artsy building with a long porch in front surrounded by a bank of red and pink hollyhocks. Colorful handmade clothing and assorted weavings hung on the porch ceiling, which was painted bright turquoise. The place was a riot of color.

Fernando walked inside the mercantile, half art gallery and half hardware store. The clerk sat on a stool behind the front counter, a thin man with long gray hair and a goatee who could have been any age between forty and sixty. He reeked of pot and had the smile to go with it. "Howdy, friend, what can I do for you on this fine sunny day?" he asked.

Fernando smiled back. "I'm looking for a friend of mine, a young fella named Jack Ryan Junior who wears a white western hat and drives a black Dodge Ram pickup. He said he's living in an old farmhouse somewhere up here. Didn't give me an address. I wonder if you've seen him or heard of anyone new who's just moved into an abandoned farmhouse."

The man with the goatee thought for a long moment, as though trying to focus, and then shook his head. "Nope. Haven't seen anyone like that here. Do you know the whereabouts of this old farmhouse?"

"No, just that it's supposed to be off grid," Fernando said. "Whatever that means. I'm still not sure."

“Hah! Pretty much everything here is off grid. You just got to turn your electronics off--hell, those things are emitting harmful rays on your brain anyway--or better yet, toss ‘em in the ditch.”

“Yeah, you might have something there, except then you’d be littering,” Fernando said.

The clerk laughed. “Good one!”

“So you haven’t noticed anyone new in town?”

“No, but if your friend’s here, he’s likely to stop in for supplies, sooner or later,” the clerk said.

Fernando handed him a card. “If you do happen to see Jack Junior, or hear of someone moving into an old abandoned farm nearby, give me a call, would you?”

The clerk nodded, examining the card. “Private investigator, eh?”

“Fernando Lopez. I’m helping the Taos County Sheriff on an ongoing investigation.”

The clerk glanced up at Fernando. “What kind of investigation would that be, if you don’t mind me asking?”

“Murder. Two people have been murdered, one in Taos and another up in Questa.”

The clerk shook his head. “No kidding? We don’t see much of that around these parts. Damn outsiders are bringing in all that violence. We’re peaceful people in Arroyo Seco.”

“Don’t I know it,” Fernando said and turned to walk away.

“Peace, brother,” the clerk said.

“Amen.”

15

Fernando drove straight to the El Pueblo, tired of the wild goose chase. He stopped by the office and re-upped for another night and then went to his room to regroup. He tried to reach Hank, but his call went directly to voicemail. So he splashed water on his sunburned face and combed his short salt and pepper hair. He shook his head at what he saw in the mirror and finally said the hell with it and went next door to Michael's Kitchen for dinner.

Afterwards he walked back to the El Pueblo, determined to rest before returning to the Sagebrush for another night of stalking Cowboy Jack. He'd just opened the door to his room when he heard Hank's cruiser turn into the parking lot, tires squealing and horn honking. Hank laid on the horn all the way to the end unit, where he pulled up next to the Cherokee.

Fernando saw Roy riding shotgun in the cruiser. He held a cane between his legs and looked exhausted.

He left the door to his room wide open and walked over to Roy's open window. "How's the leg, Roy? Are you getting around better?"

"Little bit," Roy said. "I can walk--slowly--for about half an hour without the cane. I'm trying to stretch it out every day."

Fernando looked past Roy to Hank. "So what'd you find on the mountain?"

"Hah!" Hank roared. "Ruth said Cowboy Jack had moved out, just like you said. She didn't mention Arroyo Seco, but I don't know. I'm suspicious of the whole thing. Sounds like horseshit to me."

"No sign of him?"

"None. We searched every damn building on the ranch and didn't see hide nor hair of him."

"What about Donnie?" Fernando asked.

Hank nodded. "Yeah, he was there. Hiding in his bunker. I don't know what the hell he's afraid of now that Armando's dead. Tony and little Rosalia aren't gonna cause any trouble."

"Well, I'm going back to the Sagebrush about seven. If I see Cowboy Jack I'll call you right away."

"Good," Hank said, waving. "We're headed to Michael's Kitchen for supper. Then I'll be at the office until ten."

Fernando watched them drive out of the parking and into traffic on the Paseo. The moment he stepped inside his room he saw the magic housekeeping had done to clean up the mess he'd left that morning. Slovenly didn't begin to describe his habits. At home he walked the straight and narrow, but when he was away by himself, he just never bothered to pick up things. If they were thrown all over the damn room they were in plain sight and easier to find. Simple as that.

He called Estelle and told her about his day and their lack of progress in finding Anne Lewis' killer. She didn't seem disappointed that he wouldn't be home for another day or so. She'd given up trying to keep him on a tight leash. Now that she was occupied with her work for the Saint Francis Immigrant Outreach Program, she was too busy to waste her time trying to rein him in, as she had done all those years he had worked for the Santa Fe Police Department. She'd given up. What was it she'd said the day he left for Taos? People will do what they will do. Amen.

Again the realization that they'd grown apart made him sad. He missed the closeness of their younger years, those years when they were raising a family and he was working for peanuts as a Santa Fe cop. But age had a way of separating people, no matter how close they once were.

He hated dwelling on all this. Idleness always sent him to the dark place. He needed to stay busy in order to avoid the brooding that could paralyze him.

Enough! He grabbed an extra clip of ammo from his duffel bag and slammed the door closed behind him. Once on the road he began to focus on the plan for the night. Déjà vu all over again, as Yogi Berra famously said.

He arrived at the Sagebrush shortly after seven p.m. He could hear the band playing inside the Cantina as he parked the Cherokee. He made his way into the historic building and squeezed his way through the raucous crowd. He sat at the same corner table that offered a view of the entire bar. Well-lubricated dancers stomped and twirled on the dance floor, while the serious drinkers crowded around the bar. He saw Bonnie and Jacqueline and Trevor tossing down shooters and beers. Even José, the director, was present and accounted for. He wondered if they were celebrating something, maybe the conclusion of shooting tomorrow or the day after, according to Kim.

When a server finally appeared at his table, he ordered his

usual Modelo draft. When it arrived he sipped the cold beer slowly while waiting to see if Cowboy Jack showed up to join the festivities. Halfway through his first Modelo he caught a glimpse of a familiar, but unwelcome face standing at the bar: Joe Monroe, who must have entered from the rear door to the patio. Monroe was staring at him with his usual look of hatred on his chubby face.

The sight of Monroe enraged Fernando. But he kept his cool. He pretended not to see fat man. Instead, he finished his Modelo and asked the server for another. While the server went to get the beer, Fernando stood. He watched Monroe out of the corner of his eye, standing at the table until he was sure fat man saw him. Then he made his way through the crowd, heading for the men's restroom. The restrooms were down a long dark hallway in the oldest part of the original building.

In the restroom Fernando turned on the sink faucet and moved to the side of the door, standing flat against the wall. He took out his Smith & Wessen from its open carry holster on his belt and waited. He didn't have to wait long. He heard muffled footsteps approaching and then stopping outside the restroom door. Time stopped. He could hear Monroe breathing on the other side of the door. Seconds later the door kicked open and Monroe barged in. Fat man entered with his right arm extended, Glock in hand. A serious mistake.

Fernando made him pay. He brought his Smith & Wessen down hard on Monroe's wrist. The carpal bones in the wrist cracked as the Glock bounced across the bathroom floor. Monroe screamed. He bent over, holding his right arm with his left hand, as if the right hand had been severed.

Fernando raised his leg and kicked Monroe hard, sending him crashing to the floor. Then he kicked the fallen man in the side and was about to stomp on fat man's face before he came to his senses. He needed to control his rage. Too much adrenaline can make a man do foolish things. Monroe was badly injured, that was enough. He didn't want or need to kill him.

So he stood over Monroe and pressed his Smith & Wessen against fat man's forehead for the second time. "Listen, you stupid bastard, I have nothing to do with the lawsuits against Ted Fisher! You understand? Nothing!"

Monroe made gurgling sounds on the floor.

"Tell your boss to leave me alone! This is your second warning. There won't be a third!" Fernando said, pushing the barrel of his gun hard against fat man's forehead, so hard blood began to appear around the barrel. When he saw the blood, Fernando tucked his Smith &

Wessen back in its holster and kicked Monroe in the side one more time for good measure.

Fat man yelped.

Leaving Monroe, Fernando turned off the faucet and picked up the man's Glock. He closed the bathroom door behind him and walked down the dark hallway into the unused part of the original building. Eventually he found a rear door that opened on the interior courtyard. But the door wouldn't budge, even after he unlocked it. So he continued on into the dark building until he came to a laundry room. Across the hall from the laundry room was another door, wide open, with laundry carts lined up outside on the pavement. That would do just fine.

He stepped outside and walked along the back of the building until he spotted an industrial dumpster. Looking around to make sure he didn't have company, he removed the clip from the Glock and put it in his back pocket. Then he walked over to the dumpster and tossed in the Glock. Fat man wouldn't be needing the Glock anytime soon. Not with a broken right wrist.

Fernando continued around to the front of the Sagebrush and reentered through the door to the Cantina. His corner table was still vacant, with a fresh Modelo waiting. He squeezed through the crowd and took his seat. No sign of Cowboy Jack at the bar, but everyone else seemed celebratory, laughing and tossing back drinks as fast as the bartender could serve them.

He nursed his beer as slowly as he could. He managed to stretch it out for over an hour. By ten o'clock he was dog-tired and fed up with waiting for Cowboy Jack to appear. There had to be a better way.

He left the Cantina in a worse mood than when he arrived, if that was possible. Something had to break soon or he would say the hell with it and go back to Santa Fe, where he belonged. Even if he had to abandon Hank.

When he stepped outside, he heard an angry voice yelling in the parking lot. Instinctively he reached for his Smith & Wessen. If it was Monroe, he intended to shoot the fool and be done with it, but the yell turned out to be from a drunk looking for his car, a big man wearing a torn white T-shirt and baggy khaki pants. The drunk staggered out from behind a car and mumbled something to Fernando.

"Whatever you say," Fernando said.

"Danm right," the drunk said, holding on to the parked vehicles as he moved from one row to the next, cursing all the way.

On edge, Fernando climbed into his Cherokee and drove back to the El Pueblo. Maybe a good night's sleep would help his mood, because it couldn't get any darker this side of the grave.

16

After a restless night, Fernando awoke with a new resolution. If nothing broke this morning, he would clear out by eleven o'clock, El Pueblo's departure time. He cleaned up and went to Michael's Kitchen for breakfast. When he came back to his room he picked up all his belongings, everything he'd scattered about the room and the bathroom, and stuffed them in his duffel bag. Then he sat down in his desk chair to call Hank and tell him he needed to get back to Santa Fe.

Just as he reached for his phone the damn thing rang. He didn't recognize the number but answered anyway.

"Hey, Mister Lopez, this is Pete Williams calling," a friendly voice said.

Fernando drew a blank. He couldn't remember encountering anyone named Pete Williams.

"Yeah--you gave me your card yesterday at the Mercantile--you know, Arroyo Seco? You told me to call if I saw a young feller driving a black Dodge pickup. Well, he stopped by last evening, a youngster wearing a white western hat, just like you described."

"Really? Okay, you surprised me...thanks for calling back," Fernando said. Now he remembered the pot-smoking clerk with long gray hair. "Sounds like Jack Ryan Junior. What did he want?"

"Well, he bought some tools. Shovels and a hammer and saw, even a heavy-duty push broom. Like he was fixin' to do some home repair."

"Un-huh, sounds about right," Fernando said. "Did he say where this farm of his is located?"

"No, not exactly, but I think it's the old Rodriguez homestead by the way he described it. I can tell you how to get there when you come up. It's kinda hard to find, is the thing."

"Okay, we'll be up," Fernando said and clicked off.

Fernando didn't waste any time. He called Hank immediately and told him the news.

"No shit?" was Hank's reaction. "Well, I'll be damned. So he did show up in Arroyo Seco after all. I never thought he'd leave the ranch, not in a million years. He's a mama's boy as much as he is a ladies man."

"He knows we're after him," Fernando said. "He's on the run."

Hank paused a moment. "Okay, I'll pick you up shortly. Should I bring Roy along?"

Fernando laughed. "I think the two of us can handle Cowboy Jack."

"I'm on my way."

He threw his duffel bag on the opposite bed, fully packed. He would deal with that later. He was sure to miss the checkout time, so it looked like he would be in Taos for at least one more day. He buckled on his holster and pocketed his extra clip. He couldn't think of anything else he needed to do, so he went outside and sat on the metal chair out front of his door. And waited.

When Hank drove up a few minutes later he was alone in the big cruiser. That pleased Fernando. He liked Roy, but given the deputy's limited mobility, it was better for everyone if he didn't come along.

Fernando walked to the cruiser. "You want to take the Cherokee? Sounds like this abandoned farm might be difficult to get to."

"Off grid," Hank added, laughing. "Nah, let's take the cruiser. This needs to be an official visit."

So Fernando climbed in the cruiser and buckled up, preparing for another wild ride with Hank at the wheel. The big man never slowed down. When an unsuspecting motorist got in his way, Hank honked until the motorist moved over.

The drive from the El Pueblo to the Arroyo Seco Mercantile took Hank all of ten minutes. He skidded to a stop in front of the Mercantile and set the brake.

Fernando relaxed finally. "You must have been hell on wheels when you were a teenager!"

Hank gave him the Evil Eye. "What? Are you insulting my driving?"

"Is that what you call it?" Fernando joked. "I'd call it racing."

Hank smiled. "Let's see what this Pete Williams has to say."

They climbed out of the cruiser and walked into the Mercantile, dodging the multi-colored fabrics hanging on the porch. Fernando led Hank through the aisles of clothing and tools to the counter in back.

Williams beamed when he saw them approaching. "You're back," he said to Fernando. "And you brought the law with you, I see."

Hank tipped his black Stetson. "Hank Mathews, Taos County Sheriff."

"Pleased to meet you. Like I told Mister Lopez here, the young feller you're looking for came in yesterday evening," Williams said, stroking his gray goatee. "Bought some tools and said he was staying at an old abandoned farm hereabouts. From his description I think it's the old Rodriguez place south of town."

"Was he alone?" Hank asked.

Williams shook his head. "He came in by himself, but I saw someone else sitting in the pickup."

"Man or woman?" Hank asked.

"Looked like a young man about my daughter's age. Maybe a high school student?"

"Probably his younger brother," Hank said. "So how do we find this Rodriguez place?"

Williams considered a moment before speaking. "Well, do you remember passing over El Salto Wash on your way into town?"

Hank nodded. "Sort of."

"It was kind of a blur," Fernando added. Hank gave him a dirty look.

"Okay, well go back to that bridge and look for a primitive dirt road off to the west of the bridge," Williams said. "Looks more like an animal trail than a road, but if you look close enough you'll see tire tracks. Take that road for about three miles. It runs parallel to the wash until you come to an overgrowth of trees, saltbush and willow and some juniper. You'll see a bend in the wash heading back east. Right there's where you'll find the Rodriguez farm, what's left of it. There's a shotgun house and a chicken coop and a couple of sheds, all built from slats and rough-cut wood. It ain't much to look at--nobody's lived there for over ten years."

While he spoke, a young woman wearing tights and a sweatshirt walked out of a back room and idled up to Williams. She was chewing gum and talking at the same time. "Go on, tell them the rest of the story, daddy," she said.

Williams frowned. He looked embarrassed. "This here's my daughter Mary Lynn."

"What does she mean 'the rest of the story'?" Fernando asked.

Williams stroked his goatee again. "Thing is, some say the farm's haunted. Rodriguez hung himself in the chicken coop back in the late nineties. Nineteen ninety- nine, I think. His egg and chicken raising business went bust, and then his wife and child died in a traffic accident on the highway to Taos. He was terrible depressed after that. One day he threaded a rope around one of the rafters in the chicken coop and hung himself."

Fernando glanced at Hank. He didn't like what he was hearing.

"About ten years later a young couple moved in and tried to make a go of it," Williams continued. "Couple of hippies from Taos. They tried chickens and organic gardening. But they kept catching glimpses of Rudy hanging there by a rope in the chicken coop. Or Rudy's ghost, whatever the hell it was they saw. Scared them off finally, and nobody's been willing to set foot in the place since, except maybe an occasional hunter looking for temporary shelter."

The three men were silent. Meagan walked off into the back room, still chewing her gum.

"Much obliged for the information," Hank said finally. He turned and marched out of the mercantile while Fernando followed along behind.

Hank climbed into the cruiser and slammed the door closed. Fernando did the same.

Hank turned to Fernando. "I'm not superstitious, but I sure's hell don't want to rile up a ghost."

Fernando laughed. "Isn't that a contradiction?"

"Not if you think about it," Hank said, and gunned the engine. He shot off back down Highway 150 until he came to the bridge over El Salto Wash and slammed on the brakes.

"I don't see no road," Hank said.

Fernando jumped out of the car and walked into the ditch looking for anything resembling a road. He walked west away from the bridge about 100 feet before he saw tire tracks. The tracks were difficult to see because they disappeared into a wall of weeds along the ditch.

Pointing at the tire tracks Fernando walked back to the cruiser and climbed aboard.

Hank nodded and edged the cruiser down to where Fernando pointed. The big car bounced over the lip of the highway and into the shallow ditch. The cruiser's tires spun in the soft sand but then caught and sent them careening out of the ditch and onto the primitive road. Hank cursed as he steered the cruiser first to the right and then to the left trying to avoid rocks and ruts and patches of tall weeds. He repeatedly stopped and started, stopped and started for what seemed like forever. Finally they saw a wooded area ahead, marking the bend in the wash where the abandoned farm was located, according to Williams.

The abandoned farmhouse came into view as they came closer, a tumbledown wooden structure with a tin roof. Its front door hung cockeyed from one hinge. Vandals or squatters had broken out its front windows. Across a flat patch of dirt and weeds stood the chicken coop, larger than the house but constructed from the same rough-cut wood with a slanted tin roof.

"Up there," Fernando said, pointing to a black pickup partially hidden behind a stand of trees near the wash. Next to it was some sort of bright red object. Looked like a campsite.

Hank slowed down looking for a place to park. When he spotted a thick cluster of chamisa about halfway between the pickup and the house, he pulled in behind the bushes. Then he set the brake and climbed out of the cruiser. He took the lead, with his Colt .45 in hand. Fernando followed, waiting to see what developed before he drew his Smith & Wessen.

"Jack Junior?" Hank yelled, walking toward the pickup. "Come on out, son. We're here to help you. No one's gonna get hurt."

As they rounded the bend they saw the red object was a nylon tent, erected beside a dead campfire and two folding chairs. Other camping equipment lay in the bed of the Dodge pickup. That included a Coleman camping stove, a sleeping bag, and a cooler. It looked like Cowboy Jack planned to camp out while he worked on making the farmhouse livable.

Hank turned to Fernando. "What do you wanna do? Looks like trails in the saltbush over by the wash."

Fernando shook his head. "No thanks. You walk into that stuff, you can't see ten feet ahead of you. Let's check out the house."

So they backtracked to the dilapidated house, which looked like it could collapse at any moment. The rough-cut wooden structure seemed to sink into the sand. The timbers were warped and uneven, with gaps between the thin walls and the joists supporting the roof. The front door hung from one hinge as if someone had kicked it in not long ago. Maybe the door had been locked when Cowboy Jack arrived and he'd done the damage himself.

Hank approached the door cautiously. He stepped up on a large piece of flagstone that served as a porch and stuck his head through the opcning. It took a moment for his eyes to adjust to the darkness. When they did, he entered the dark ruin with his Colt .45 out front. He immediately sneezed. "Shit! Dusty in here."

Fernando followed and saw why. Cowboy Jack had been sweeping the floors with the push broom he bought at Arroyo Seco Mercantile. Piles of dirt lay on the floor, with the broom resting against the kitchen sink. As a consequence the air inside was clotted with dust. He saw a galaxy of dust mites in the ray of light splashing through the one broken window in the room.

Fernando waved the air in front of his face, as if that would help him breathe. Through the dust he saw a gallon bottle of water and plastic cups resting on the kitchen counter. Not much else, except a roll of plastic sheeting along with duct tape and a staple gun placed on the kitchen table. That would be supplies to cover the broken windows and front door, Fernando supposed. Otherwise the room was totally empty, as were the two tiny bedrooms off the front room. Except, that is, for piles of trash on the floor of all three rooms.

He followed Hank outside, coughing.

Hank didn't waste any time. He headed directly across the dirt yard to the chicken coop, built out of the same rough-cut wood as the house but more intact. The remnants of hay and straw bales lay scattered around the front of the coop. Hank opened the heavy wooden door and stepped inside, still holding his Colt .45. He stopped immediately and cursed. "Stinks in here!"

Fernando glanced around the yard, looking for Cowboy Jack. When he didn't see Cowboy, he joined Hank inside the coop. The door swung closed behind him. The coop smelled like a mixture of hay and chickens and chicken shit. Only thing missing were the chickens, but there was enough chicken shit smeared over every surface in the coop to make up for the missing chickens. The plank floor, the nesting boxes, and the roosting bars were literally covered in dried, powdery white chicken shit and stank to high heaven. The watering and feeding platforms were even worse.

Fernando noticed a rope still hanging from the rafters. Whoever cut down Rodriguez hadn't bothered to take down the rope. That struck him as bizarre. Why keep the rope? A reminder?

Hank surveyed the coop. "Reminds me of my granddaddy's chickens. I remember having to gather eggs as a kid. God, I hated them stinkin' chickens."

"Yeah? I'll spare you my childhood barnyard memories, if you'll spare me yours."

Hank shot him a dirty look.

Just then Fernando smelled something that caused him to stop. "Wait. What's that smell? Gasoline?"

They both turned and made for the door. Too late.

Suddenly they heard an explosion that sounded like a shotgun blast. Instantly fire engulfed the front of the coop and blinded them. Aided by the highly combustible hay and straw mixture outside, the rough-cut wood burned fast--and hot. So hot it singed their eyebrows and made their eyes water from ten feet away.

They covered their faces with their arms and backed away from the door as it burst into flames. Out of the corner of his eye Fernando thought he saw a black object, a body, swinging from the rope above.

Was it his imagination? Smoke began to fill the coop, obscuring his vision and poisoning the air. He started to cough, the smoke was choking him.

They had to get out fast. They had only seconds. But how?

Then Fernando saw a possible way out. He grabbed Hank and pulled him toward the chicken chute at the back of the coop. The swinging door that allowed chickens to go in or out might provide an escape route if it was large enough.

Hank fought him at first, but then he saw what Fernando had in mind. He tucked his Colt back in its holster and grabbed his Stetson. Then he pushed Fernando forward, wanting him to go first.

Fernando fell to his knees and crawled up the ramp to the swinging door. Coughing, he plunged his head through the door and gasped for air. Then he pulled himself out of the burning building and slid down the ramp outside. When he turned around he saw Hank toss his black Stetson outside first and then stick his head through the door. Problem was, his shoulders were too big. He couldn't get his body through the opening. His big hands flopped helplessly outside the door.

"Shit! Shit!" Fernando shouted. He grabbed both of Hank's hands and pulled as hard as he could. Hank yelled for him to stop, but he kept pulling anyway.

Finally one shoulder popped out of the opening, and then the other shoulder. Suddenly Hank came sliding down the ramp like an avalanche, colliding with Fernando. The two of them lay on the ground gasping for air.

At that instant the entire building exploded in fire, sending flames and sparks high in the air. The scene turned surreal. They lay on their backs watching bits of burning material float down on top of them, covering the ground and everything on it with flaming ash. Areas of dead grass around them began to smolder.

Fernando and Hank crawled away on their hands and knees until they reached the wash behind the coop. They plunged over the lip of the wash and fell to the bottom, landing in the soft sand.

Hank lay in the sand for a moment and then realized he didn't have his Stetson. Cursing, he scrambled up the side of the wash and looked over at the burning coop. By now flames had engulfed the entire coop, including the ramp. His black hat lay a few feet away from the burning ramp. Hank moved quickly, hoisting himself over the lip of the wash and dashing over to grab his hat. He examined the Stetson and then shook it, as if shaking out fire. Then he popped the Stetson on his head and walked back to the wash, looking down on Fernando, who hadn't moved.

"Jesus Christ, you're covered in chicken shit," Hank said to Fernando.

Fernando sat up and looked at himself. As Hank said, his clothing was covered in dried white chicken shit. His only solace was that Hank looked every bit as besmirched as he did. Even worse.

"Hah, you should see yourself," Fernando replied.

Hank nodded. "I don't know about you, but I'm gettin' mighty pissed at Cowboy Jack," Hank said. "I've known him since he was a damn kid, and now look at the grief he's causing me."

"Grief? He tried to kill us!" Fernando said.

Just then they heard a vehicle driving back up the dirt road toward the bridge.

"There he goes," Hank said. "I'm thinking maybe I should have shot him back on the mountain when I had the chance. Save me a whole lotta trouble."

Fernando was thinking the same thing.

Hank glanced down at Fernando. "Are you gonna sit there all day or what?"

"What are my choices?" Fernando asked.

"Good, bad, and ugly."

Fernando managed to get to his feet and salute Hank. A mock salute. He brushed the worst of the ash and chicken shit off his clothing and then climbed out of the wash. Then he followed Hank back to the cruiser. From there they watched the coop burn down to a heap of black, smoldering embers.

Hank pointed to the trees.

Over where Cowboy Jack's pickup had been parked, the red tent and folding chairs were long gone. Cowboy Jack was on the run. Again.

17

Before leaving Hank called his office and had them send out an APB for the black Dodge Ram pickup. Afterwards they climbed into the cruiser and drove back to Arroyo Seco. Their first stop was the Mercantile, where Pete Williams greeted them from behind the counter. Williams laughed at their bedraggled appearance, their clothing streaked with white powder and their faces smudged black from the smoke. "Whoa... what happened to you fellers?" he asked.

Hank growled but said nothing.

When they got closer Williams sniffed a couple of times and said, "Wait, what's that I smell? Smoke and something else?" He stuck his head over the counter to get a closer whiff.

"Chicken shit," Hank said. "From the chicken coop at the Rodriguez farm. The guy we're after set it on fire--with us inside."

Williams looked at them wide-eyed and speechless.

"So you better call the local fire department," Hank continued. "They'll need to make sure the fire doesn't spread to the mesa. Some of the grass along the wash is drier than all get out. Okay?"

Williams nodded, reaching for the phone. "Will do. There's not much down there, but a grass fire could spread if the wind picks up."

While Williams called, Hank and Fernando walked outside. Hank leaned back against the cruiser and folded his arms over his chest. "What do you think? Do we wait for the APB to produce results, or do we go up that damn mountain again to look for Cowboy Jack?"

Fernando joined him leaning on the cruiser. "Well, if he didn't go back to the ranch, where would he go?"

Hank didn't answer.

"I hate to say it, but I suppose we should check the ranch first," Fernando said, shaking his head in disgust.

Hank spit and kicked at the gravel on the side of the road. "Then we'll have to go all the way back to Taos. Unfortunately there ain't no direct way to get to Questa from Arroyo Seco."

Fernando shrugged.

"Okay, let's do it, what the hell," Hank said. He looked down at his smudged and streaked uniform. "You think we should clean up first?"

"What's the point?" Fernando asked.

Hank grumbled something and climbed into the cruiser. Fernando did the same. When they drove off, Fernando noticed Pete Williams watching from the window of his Mercantile. Fernando wasn't sure, but Williams seemed to be laughing at them. Just what Williams found funny escaped him.

Hank drove back to the junction with Highway 522 just outside of Taos and then turned right to Questa. They stopped at a gas station in Questa for bottles of water and hot dogs that looked like they'd been roasting on the spittle for a month. Tasted like it too. Fernando spit his out in the parking lot, but Hank devoured his dog as if he hadn't eaten in a month. Not stopping there, Hank sopped up the remaining ketchup on his paper plate with the last bit of white bun and then belched. Loudly.

Fernando held his tongue. He watched while Hank finished his bottle of water and then tossed the plastic bottle out of his window, aiming for a trash receptacle nearby. He missed.

Then they tore off, weaving through the curves on Cabresto Canyon Road. Hank slowed down when he came to the dirt road leading to the Ryan Ranch. Fortunately the metal gate across the road was open, so Hank gunned the big engine and roared up to Donnie's bunker, kicking up a trail of dust. He parked a good distance away from the house and barn to give them room to maneuver in case Cowboy Jack popped out of one of the buildings and started shooting. Even with his right hand bandaged from Hank's bullet, Cowboy Jack could be dangerous.

The first thing Fernando noticed after the dust settled was that Cowboy Jack's black Dodge pickup was not in the yard.

The second thing he noticed was Ruth Ryan sitting in a rocking chair on the porch. When she saw them get out of the cruiser she bolted up out of the chair and stormed off the porch. It didn't look like she was planning a friendly greeting. Sure enough, she grabbed the pistol in her shoulder holster and waved it over her head. Not a good sign.

"Oh shit," Hank said, walking toward the house. "Now old Ruth's all riled up. Watch out, she's a tiger."

"Damn you to hell, Hank Mathews, you drove off both my boys!" she shouted. "I could kill you!"

Ruth fired off two shots. The bullets zinged above their heads.

Fernando crouched behind the cruiser, not about to take any

chances, even though Ruth didn't appear to be much of a shot. Hank, on the other hand, did not take shelter. Too proud. Instead, he continued walking out in the open with his hands up in the air. "Now, calm down, Ruth," Hank said. "I've known you and Jack Senior for a long time. I've been a friend of your family longer'n I can remember. You know that as well as I do."

"You're no friend! Not any more! You took away my boys!" Ruth shouted, and fired off a couple more rounds. The bullets kicked up dust in front of Hank and ricocheted down the drive.

"Jesus, woman, will you stop shooting!" Hank shouted back. "I'm trying to help your boys, goddamnit!"

"Liar!" she shouted and fired again. Twice.

"Owww! Shit!" Hank shouted, and danced a jig. "You hit my foot!"

"Good!" Ruth yelled and pulled the trigger again. They all heard a dry click. She was out of ammunition. Thank God.

Hank grabbed his left foot and cursed up a storm.

"Stay right there," Ruth said. "I'm going in the house for more bullets, but I'll be right back to shoot you again."

"Stop! Wait a dang moment, let's talk," Hank shouted and walk/hopped toward Ruth, who stood her ground, daring Hank to come closer. "Please, Ruth! Let me say what I come to say."

She looked him in the eye. "Hah! If I had another bullet in the chamber I'd shoot you in that big fat belly of yours."

"Okay, I understand why you're angry at me, but please, let me explain," Hank pleaded.

Ruth stared at Hank. She seemed to really 'see' him for the first time. "What in God's name happened to you anyway?"

Hank laughed. "We had a little trouble with a chicken house."

"Was there a fire? You smell like smoke."

"Yes, ma'am. The damned thing burned down. With us in it."

"Yeah, well you smell like you just came from a chicken barbecue--and you were the chickens!"

Hank laughed again.

Ruth frowned and put her pistol back in its holster. "So what do you have to say to me, Hank Mathews?"

"Well, dammit, I'll tell you, if you stop shooting at me," Hank said. "I need to talk to Jack Junior. I'm trying to stop this damn feud. The only way I can see to do it is to charge Jack Junior for the murder of Armando and let it all come out in a court of law, the whole kit and caboodle. He'll claim self-defense, that Armando shot first, and there's not a shred of hard evidence to contradict him. But the killing has to stop, and the only way to do that is to bring all the hotheads together in court and read them the riot act. Give Jack Junior a taste of jail, and maybe little Tony Lucero too if he tries to get back at Jack, which I don't think he'll do because he and his little sis Rosalia have more sense than the older siblings. Same thing with Donnie...I hope."

"What do you mean? He'll have to go to jail?" Ruth asked.

"Only until you bail him out," Hank said. "I'm telling you, just find yourself a good lawyer and everything will work out."

Fernando stepped forward. He took out his pocket notebook and wrote a name on a slip of paper. "Here," he said, handing the paper to Ruth. "You need to call Raoul Garcia in Santa Fe. He's the best criminal lawyer in the state. He virtually never loses a case. This should be an easy one for him."

"In Santa Fe?" Ruth asked. "Would he come all this way?"

"Yes, ma'am, Raoul travels all over the state," Fernando said. "His nickname is 'Guilty Man Walking' because all his clients are guilty and they all get off."

She took the note and nodded. "Well, I suppose...."

"So tell me truly, is Jack Junior hiding here?" Hank asked.

"No, I told you, he came and got Donnie earlier today and the two of them took off. They got all their camping equipment in the pickup. I don't know where they went."

Hank looked her in the eye. "Are you telling me the truth?"

"Yes, I'm telling you the truth. What are you, hard of hearing?"

Hank and Fernando both laughed. Ruth laughed too.

"Okay, then," Hank said. "Tell Jack Junior what I said, and tell him to turn himself in so we can finish this nasty business. There's been too much killing."

Skeptical, Ruth nodded begrudgingly.

Hank turned and hobbled back to the cruiser favoring his left foot. He opened the driver's door and started to climb in but then thought twice about it and stopped. Instead, he walked around the cruiser and climbed in the passenger's seat, riding shotgun.

Fernando waited a moment to see if Hank would change his mind. He'd never seen Hank ride shotgun. Ever.

Hank turned around and yelled, "What are you waiting for? Let's get the hell out of here."

With that, Fernando climbed into the driver's seat and waited for Hank to give him the keys, which he did. Reluctantly.

"So, Sundance, why didn't you return fire?" Fernando asked, joking.

"I couldn't shoot Ruth," Hank said. "Come on, she's a distraught mother."

"That she is," Fernando said.

As they drove off, Hank said, "Take me to the ER. That crazy bitch shot me in the foot."

18

Their late afternoon trip to the Holy Cross Emergency Room turned out to be a nightmare. They spent three hours waiting for an exam room, surrounded by crying children and homeless vagabonds who reeked of booze, and then another hour waiting for a nurse, not to mention a doctor. To make matters worse, they ended up with one of the nurses who attended Fernando when Joe Monroe knocked him unconscious in the hallway of the Sagebrush.

"You two again, eh? Are you seeing double or feeling faint?" she asked Fernando, a no-nonsense middle-aged woman with premature gray hair and thick glasses. She reached for a stethoscope.

"I'm okay, he's the one with the problem today," Fernando said, pointing to Hank sitting on the exam table.

"Well, I wondered what you were doing up there," the nurse said. "What's wrong with you, sheriff?"

Hank pointed to his left foot.

The nurse sniffed at the strange odor in the tight exam room. Then she zeroed in on their clothing. "What happened to you guys? You look--I don't know--like the homeless people we have out front."

"It's a long story," Hank said.

The nurse looked at Hank's chart. "Says here you were shot in the left foot. Is that correct?"

Hank held up his left leg. His boot had a slash along one side from the toe to the heel. Looked like a knife had slit it open.

The nurse bent over and tried to pull off the boot. Not a good move. Hank cursed and hollered until she stopped and brought in an orderly to help. While the orderly held Hank's foot steady, the nurse cut off the boot with a scalpel and scissors. Then she pulled down the blood-soaked sock and tossed it in a trash receptacle. "Hmmm," she said, holding the foot in her hand.

Moments later the doctor came into the exam room, a tall beanpole of a man wearing a white jacket. He looked at the foot and said, "You're a lucky man, Mr. Mathews. The bullet missed the bone. You just have a nasty laceration there, and part of your little toe is missing, but the nurse can close the wound with liquid sutures. No stitches will be required. Your foot will be sore for a week or two, but it should mend just fine."

The doctor shook Hank's hand, as if Hank had just won the lottery. Then he disappeared, not to return.

The nurse cleaned the wound, applied the liquid sutures, and gently bandaged the foot.

"How the hell am I supposed to walk with my foot bandaged like that?" Hank asked the nurse.

The nurse laughed. "We'll give you a medical boot to wear on that foot. It's like a bloated sandal. You can wear it for a week or so, until the foot feels better. I'll be right back with the boot."

A few minutes later she returned with the medical boot and showed Hank how to put it on. "You're free to go," she said.

Hank limped to the front desk, signed the appropriate papers, and then limped outside to the cruiser. Fernando followed.

Outside the sun was already setting in the western sky, the mountains to the north starting to disappear in shadows. The day was all but shot.

"Do you want me to drive?" Fernando asked.

"No sir, I got to get used to this damn boot," Hank said. "I might as well start now. Good thing it's my left foot."

Hank fired up the engine and drove through town to the El Pueblo. With his big foot he drove slower than usual at first. Which was fine with Fernando, never a big fan of Hank's driving.

Hank's extra caution lasted all of five minutes. By the time they reached the Plaza intersection he was speeding in and out of lanes and honking at slower vehicles to get out of his way

At the El Pueblo Hank squealed to a stop beside the Cherokee. "I'll let you know as soon as we get results from the APB."

Fernando paused before getting out of the cruiser. "You realize... when you talked to Ruth, that you didn't mention Cowboy Jack's possible involvement in the murder of Anne Lewis."

Hank nodded. "I just didn't want to overload her. Pile on all the possible charges facing Cowboy Jack. Didn't seem like a good idea. We can appraise her of that later, when she calms down a bit. Plus, I wanted to get the hell out of there without getting killed."

"You think she'll take it any better later on if Cowboy gets charged?" Fernando asked.

Hank smiled. "Probably not. I'll be sure to wear my bullet proof vest."

With that Hank drove off fast, squealing out of the parking lot and onto the Paseo. It was becoming more apparent that his medical boot and wounded foot hadn't changed Hank's driving.

Fernando went inside his room and checked his phone calls and email messages. Nothing from Estelle or anyone else. When he entered the bathroom, he got a good look at himself in the mirror. Shocked, he stood there staring at an old man whose clothes were covered in chicken shit and whose face was blackened by smoke from the chicken coop fire back in Arroyo Seco. The sight unnerved him. He felt both humbled and angry at Cowboy Jack for leading them on a wild goose chase and then attempting to burn them alive in the chicken coop.

What also angered and surprised Fernando was that Hank was being much too lenient on Cowboy and his mother, Ruth. Not only did Cowboy shoot and kill Armando, he attempted to kill them. Plus, he happened to be the leading suspect in the Anne Lewis murder. He needed to be in jail on all three counts.

Grumbling to himself, he took off his clothes and stuffed them in a plastic laundry bag he found in the closet. Then he showered, taking his time scrubbing off the smoke and the stink. He felt like a new man when he stepped out of the shower and dressed in clean clothes. That lifted his spirits, so he went next door to Michael's Kitchen and ordered his favorite meal, cheese enchiladas with red chile and posole. Then, since the evening was young, he decided to pay yet another visit to the Sagebrush. What else did he have to do?

He drove across town to the Sagebrush and parked in his usual spot. As he switched off the engine he realized he was becoming more obsessive-compulsive as he aged. He had to park in the same spot. He had to take the same route to wherever he was going. Repetition had become his way of eliminating cognitive dissonance. Why vary? Stick to the routine, the tried and true.

He heard rockabilly music blasting from the loudspeakers inside the Cantina when he stepped out of the Cherokee. A new band, even louder than the previous group. He kind of liked the sound. At least it was familiar.

Fernando walked into the Cantina and squeezed through the crowd. He headed automatically for his corner table but was disappointed to see a young couple sitting at the table. They seemed to be engaged in an intense conversation. He stood there fidgeting for a moment and then said the hell with it and walked to the bar. He fought for elbowroom with a couple of louts in nylon jogging suits who'd had too much to drink. The beefy bartender intervened finally, telling the louts to make room for a senior citizen, meaning him.

Now that pissed him off, but he thanked the bartender anyway.

"What can I get you, young fella?" the bartender then joked.

Fernando ordered his usual Modelo. He was sipping his Modelo and minding his own business when he got a whiff of strong perfume behind him. He turned around to find an attractive young woman with short blue hair and a silver ring in one eyebrow. Bonnie Alvarez.

"Why, Mister Lopez, I didn't know you were a drinking man," she said, smiling.

"Never touch the stuff," Fernando said.

"So I see. Can I join you?"

Fernando made room at the bar. "What are you drinking?"

"Margarita, please," she said.

He called over the bartender and ordered a margarita for the lady.

Bonnie sighed. "It's been a long day. But the good news is that we're almost done shooting. Some touch up work tomorrow and then we're outta here. I can't wait to get back home."

"So that's what you're celebrating," Fernando said.

Bonnie laughed. "Yep, the awakened dead of Taos are going back to being just plain dead, and we're going back to L.A."

Fernando smiled.

To him, being dead and living in L.A were not all that different.

19

Fernando awoke with a nasty hangover. He hadn't had a hangover this bad since the last time he visited Taos, when he was investigating murders at the Painted Skull Ranch. Last night, what he remembered anyway, seemed like a dream. Like it never happened. It was so out of character for him to stand at a bar drinking one draught of Modelo after another, more than he cared to remember. Not only that, but he'd actually danced with Bonnie Alvarez. Must have been about eleven o'clock when she dragged him out on the dance floor to trip the lights fantastic. He couldn't claim to be another John Travolta, but he'd comported himself well enough. Though in retrospect he must have looked like a damn fool twirling around the dance floor with a young woman half his age. Not to mention her blue hair and eyebrow ring.

Once he brewed a cup of coffee and popped a Tylenol he started to feel better. Last night had been a well-needed distraction from chasing Cowboy Jack. He didn't regret any of it.

After breakfast at Michael's Kitchen, he walked down to the Plaza for exercise. The bright blue sky and fresh mountain air cleared his head. He changed his mind about returning to Santa Fe. Given Hank's injury, he couldn't very well abandon him now. At least not until Hank could walk without the medical boot. He found a bench in the sun and sat down, closing his eyes and letting the sunshine wash over him. He could almost fall asleep he was so relaxed.

His cell phone rang just as his eyelids started to feel heavy. He didn't have to look at the screen to know who it was.

"Fernando, we know where Cowboy Jack is," Hank said. "Or we will know, as soon as Ruth gets here. She's on her way to the office now. She wants to talk to us before giving us Cowboy's location."

Fernando laughed. "You sure she's not coming down to take another shot at you?"

Silence at the other end.

"Damn! I never thought of that," Hank said finally.

"I'm joking," Fernando said.

"Oh. Okay. Because she sounded sincere," Hank replied.

"I'm on my way," Fernando said and clicked off.

He hurried back to his room at the El Pueblo. Wasting no time, he attached his open carry holster to his belt and locked the door on the way out. Then he climbed into his Cherokee and drove down the Paseo to the sheriff's office on Lovato Place. As he pulled up in front he saw Hank peeking out the side window. Looked like Hank was waiting to see if Ruth Ryan was packing when she arrived before deciding whether to open the door.

Amused, Fernando walked into the station. He found Hank bent over staring out the window. Roy and Sally were back in Hank's office hunkered down behind the desk. Roy had his service revolver in hand.

"Hey--I was kidding," Fernando said.

Hank ignored him. "Here she is. Go on back. I'll let you know if it's safe to come out."

From the window Fernando saw the blue Honda CRV they'd seen at the Ryan ranch turning into the front parking lot. "Whatever you say," Fernando said and walked on back.

Roy and Sally greeted Fernando when he joined them in Hank's office. Sally rolled her eyes. "This is supposed to be the county sheriff's office. Why are we hiding behind a desk?"

Roy shrugged.

"She's clean!" Hank yelled from the front of the office.

Moments later Ruth walked through the door, dressed in jeans and a Mexican embroidered shirt. Her short hair was tousled every which way as if she'd just climbed out of bed and didn't give a damn how she looked. She stood in the door frowning, her usual look. What was unusual was that she'd come without her shoulder holster. She was unarmed for a change.

"Mornin' Ruth," Hank greeted her at the door.

"Don't morning me, Hank Mathews," she said. "I been depressed ever since your visit. Now you got me worried about my boys. I realize I can't protect them myself, I need your help."

"What changed your mind?" Hank asked.

"The Luceros changed my mind, that's who," Ruth said. "They came over at dusk last night and shot four of my horses. Dead."

"Shit!" Hank said. "Must be Tony. I didn't think he'd get involved."

"Well he did," Ruth said. "We need to stop this now, before there's more killing. When Jack Junior finds out the Luceros killed his horse, he'll be over there shooting everything in sight. We got to stop it."

Hank opened his arms. "That's what I've been telling you all along and what I've been trying to do."

"Well, you're doing a piss poor job, Hank," she said.

That took Hank by surprise. "What would you have me do? Tell me."

"I want you to arrest Jack Junior, like you said, and lock him up for as long as it takes for him to cool down. That's gonna be the only way to keep him from killing and getting killed. You hear me?"

"I hear you, Ruth," Hank said. "So tell me where Jack Junior's hiding. If I can find him, I can lock him up for a while and keep him safe."

Ruth reared back and gave Hank the Evil Eye. "Here's my deal. I'll tell you where he's hiding, but only on one condition." She stared at him, waiting for him to respond.

"What's the condition?"

"That you make sure he doesn't get hurt," she said, pointing a finger at Hank. "I'm counting on you to keep him safe. If one hair on his body gets hurt, I'm blaming you. And I swear on the Almighty God I will drive back down here with my pistol and shoot you. That goes for Donnie too. You understand?"

Hank sighed. "I understand. Is Donnie with Jack Junior right now?"

Ruth nodded.

Hank shook his head.

"What's the matter?" she asked.

"The more people with guns, the more likely someone will get hurt," Hank said. "That's what's the matter. Now tell me, where the hell are they? I can't help them if I don't know where they're hiding."

Ruth glanced at Hank's office where Roy, Sally, and Fernando were huddled behind the desk listening to the conversation. She scowled at them. "They're at Ghost Ranch."

"Ghost Ranch," Hank repeated.

Ruth continued. "I don't know if they're staying in one of the cabins or camping. They have camping gear in the back of their pickup. I know there's at least one campground at Ghost Ranch, maybe more."

Hank nodded.

"So I want you to find them and bring them back and protect them," Ruth said. "That's the deal."

"Okay, I'll try, Ruth," Hank said. "But if they start shooting, I can't promise–"

She raised her hand and cut him off. "No more. Don't make me regret my decision to tell you. You protect them, Hank Mathews. I'm holding you responsible for whatever happens."

With that she turned and walked out the door.

Hank followed her to the door and watched her drive away in her CRV. Then he limped into his office grumbling to himself.

Fernando noticed Hank did not have the medical boot on his left foot. Instead, he had what appeared to be an oversized hiking boot that matched the smaller hiking boot on his right foot.

"You got rid of the medical boot," Fernando said.

"Yeah, I bought a pair of hiking boots two sizes larger than my usual. Now I'm wearing one size eleven and one size thirteen. So if Ruth comes back and shoots me in my other foot, I got it covered."

20

Ghost Ranch did, indeed, have more than one campground. Fernando remembered at least two from his most recent visit, when he was chasing accused murderer Jimmy Mackey around Ghost Ranch before Jimmy himself was murdered later in Taos. Back then he vowed he would never return to Ghost Ranch. He had too many bad memories among that scattering of tumbledown buildings--casitas, bunkhouses, mess halls, museums and all the damn horse corrals for guests staying at the ranch.

Most folks around Abiquiu considered Ghost Ranch haunted. If he remembered correctly the rumors began in the 1880s when the owners, the Archuleta Brothers, named the property *Rancho de los Brujos*. The brothers, notorious cattle rustlers, stole cattle and horses from their neighbors and hid them in the box canyon behind the ranch. They chose the name Ranch of the Witches to scare away farmers and ranchers who came looking for their stolen livestock. Rumor had it the brothers murdered those who came searching for their animals and buried the bodies in the canyon or tossed them into wells.

Ghost stories soon followed. Locals claimed to hear the voices of murdered victims in the howling winds blowing through the canyon. Some saw strange lights moving inside the buildings, especially in "Ghost House," the casita where the brothers had lived. Predictably, both Archuleta Brothers met a grisly fate. One brother killed the other during an argument over booty. The surviving brother died soon after, hung by an angry posse for a life of cattle rustling and murder. Their voices joined those of the other ghosts. Or so the stories would have you believe.

Now Fernando found himself headed back to *Rancho de los Brujos*. He and Hank were supposed to arrest--or save, according to Ruth-- Cowboy Jack and Donnie. That was a new one: arrest as a means of saving someone.

Ghost Ranch, just north of Abiquiu, might not be far from Taos as the crow flies, but it took forever by highway. Hank nixed the most direct route going back to Española and then up Highway 84 because he refused to drive through Española, which he referred to as a shithole. Instead, their drive to Abiquiu led them from one minor road to another and became a mishmash of highway numbers: 68, 570, 567, 285, 111, 554, to 84. To make matters worse Hank took a wrong turn going from 111 to 554 and then another turning on 110 instead of staying on 554. By the time they reached Abiquiu it was already past noon and both of them were fit to be tied.

"You see?" Fernando asked. "It would have been a hell of a lot easier if you had gone through Española."

"Never!" Hank said. "I hate that damned place."

They passed through Abiquiu, the mesa-top village made famous by Georgia O'Keeffe, and a few minutes later arrived at Ghost Ranch. Hank turned right on the gravel road leading into the sprawling property surrounded by distant mesas and jagged cliffs. The road curved around toward the massive Kitchen Mesa, with a maze of roads connecting the various buildings off to the left. Hank steered into a parking lot in front of the Welcome Center.

Fernando didn't wait for Hank. He jumped out as soon as the cruiser came to a stop. He needed to stretch and walk around. His legs were stiff and his lower back had started to bark after the hours-long trip from hell.

Fernando surveyed the ramshackle wooden building with wings and add-ons jutting out in myriad directions. On the long porch a couple of old timers wearing western hats sat on a bench jawing.

Fernando led the way, walking up the steps and into a dark hallway, his shoes echoing on the plank floor. The rough-cut wood and western décor made you feel like you were walking back in time a hundred years.

Behind a counter at the end of the hallway stood an elderly man. His full white beard made him look like Ernest Hemingway. The Hemingway lookalike wore a leather vest with an American flag pin on its front.

"Howdy friend," the clerk said. "Can I help you?"

Hank came limping up behind Fernando. He showed the man his credentials. "We're looking for a couple of young men driving a black Dodge Ram pickup. One's in his early twenties, the other one's in his teens. They may be renting or maybe camping, we're not sure which."

The clerk looked them over. "No sir, the description doesn't ring a bell. What are their names?"

"Jack and Donnie Ryan," Hank said. "Clean cut young men. They told their mama they were staying here."

"Are they in trouble with the law?" the clerk asked, eying Hank.

"We don't know yet," Fernando added. "If they are, we're trying to make sure they don't get into any more trouble. Their mother wants us to bring them back home safe and sound."

The clerk smiled. "I know it ain't easy keeping them young fellers out of trouble. Whereabouts do they live?"

"The family has a ranch up near Questa," Fernando said.

"Well, let me see what I can find," the clerk said. He hit a few keys on his computer, scrolled down and hit a few more keys. "I don't see anyone named Ryan, but we have two young fellers in casita number three, Rick Love and Cliff Brandt. That's way down the road here past the Arts Center and the Upper Campground. It's right next to the old Bath House at the end of the road. Just in case your two guys checked in under false names." He handed Hank a colored map of Ghost Ranch.

Hank nodded.

"You can see the casita on the map here," the clerk said, pointing to a dot on the map.

Hank took his reading glasses out of his shirt pocket and glanced at the map.

"Thing is, if those two in casita number three aren't the boys you're looking for, that don't mean the Ryans aren't here," the clerk continued. "If they're camping, they might be in the big campground up on the mesa. That's pretty much a free-for-all. Hell, some campers don't even bother to register with us before they go up on the mesa. There's roads going off into the hills every which way. There's no way for us to keep track of who all's up there."

"Okay. Much obliged," Hank said.

The clerk smiled. "Good luck. I hope you get them boys back to their mama safe and sound."

Fernando followed a limping Hank outside. The old timers on the porch were still jawing.

The older of the two geezers waved. He wore a squashed straw hat and overalls. "Howdy, sheriff. You're about a hundred years too late. The Archuleta Brothers are both dead."

He and the other old timer laughed at the joke.

Smiling, Hank picked up the challenge and limped over to their bench. "The hell you say. You know what I think? If you're just reading the news now, you're the one who's too late."

"What happened to your foot?" the second old timer asked." Looks like one foot's bigger than the other."

"Long story short--I got shot."

"Must have been a piss poor shot," old timer number one said.

The two old timers laughed again.

Hank got serious for a moment. "By the way, have either of you seen a black Dodge Ram pickup with a couple of young punks driving?"

"Yeah, we saw them late yesterday afternoon," number two said. "They stopped to get a map and then drove off thataway." He pointed east toward the casitas. "Hard to forget that big black pickup. They sure make 'em big these days. Looked brand new to me."

"Thanks for the information," Hank said, and tipped his hat. "You boys have a good day."

Fernando followed Hank to the cruiser. Once inside Hank turned and asked, "What do you think? Should we stop by casita number three?"

"Might as well," Fernando said.

Hank handed Fernando the map of Ghost Ranch. "Direct me."

"Just follow the inner loop east and then turn left at the Cantina," Fernando said.

Past the Cantina they came to a small grassy campground that was largely deserted at the moment, with only two tents and a small trailer occupying campsites. Beyond the campground they entered a circle drive that took them left to a parking lot. Below the parking lot was a building labeled 'Bath House.' Above the parking lot on a small rise were nine numbered casitas all in a row--tiny structures that looked like play houses.

Fernando pointed to a white Toyota Rav4 parked in space number three.

"Yeah, we're probably wasting our time, but what the hell, we're here now," Hank said, climbing out of the cruiser. "I suppose Cowboy Jack could have swapped his Ram pickup for a Rav4."

"I doubt that," Fernando said, joining Hank.

Fernando led the way, climbing a narrow trail to the casitas. Nine casitas, exactly alike. Each of the dilapidated little structures had a bare light bulb over its door and an old metal chair on its slab concrete porch.

Fernando walked up to number three and pounded on the door.

Moments later the door opened and a young man wearing shorts and a Ball State T-shirt appeared. His long hair was tousled, as though he'd just woken up from a nap.

"Yes?" the youngster asked.

"We're looking for a couple of brothers staying at Ghost Ranch, Jack and Donnie Ryan," Fernando explained. "We thought the two of you might be the brothers. Guess we were wrong."

"Uhhh, yeah," the young man said. "I'm Rick. Cliff's out hiking on Kitchen Mesa."

Hank limped up to the concrete slab porch. "You haven't seen a black Dodge Ram pickup nearby, have you?"

Rick shook his head.

"Sorry to bother you," Fernando said, turning away. He brushed by Hank on his way down the trail to the parking lot. Like everything else these past few days, finding the Ryans was going to be more difficult than he imagined.

Fernando slammed the door of the cruiser and waited for Hank, who shuffled down the rise and climbed into the driver's seat of the cruiser.

"Tell me, what the hell is Ball State?" Hank said.

Fernando laughed. "Some college in the middle of nowhere, I think. Maybe Illinois or Indiana, one of those states up there."

"Speaking of the middle of nowhere," Hank said, looking from side to side. "I guess we need to find the big campground on the mesa, where campers go off into the hills. You got the map, my friend."

Fernando studied the map, which was anything but clear. "First, head back toward the Cantina."

Hank followed Fernando's directions. Halfway to the Cantina they turned right on a circle road that wound its way through a congested, confusing sector of casitas, public buildings, and parking lots. At the Upper Pavilion the road veered northwest and climbed a hill to the larger of the two Ghost Ranch campgrounds, surrounded by hills and receding mesas.

The open, sprawling campground spread out into the hills, crowded with brightly colored tents and trailers of various shapes and sizes. It looked like a tent city as they approached, much more active than the small campground below. They drove around the circumference of the campground on another circle road and then criss-crossed the interior roads, looking for the Ryans. They saw several red tents but none belonging to the Ryans. Nor did they see Cowboy Jack's black pickup. Most of the campers appeared to be off hiking, horseback riding, or pursuing other activities in the many public buildings on the Ghost Ranch grounds.

Hank pulled over beside a building labeled 'Bath and Laundry' and killed the engine. They climbed out of the cruiser and looked around. From the hilltop campground they had a view of the surrounding mesas, pink and white and etched into jagged cliffs by a network of arroyos that cut through the mesas. Hiking paths and primitive roads spilled out of the campground and into the rough terrain. It was the kind of landscape that provided a perfect place for people to disappear and never be seen again. Or for fugitives to hide out for however long they needed--fugitives like the Ryan brothers and before them the Archuleta Brothers.

Hank pawed at the sandy earth with his good foot and then turned to Fernando. "What are you thinking?"

Fernando ignored Hank. He went back to the cruiser and fetched his binoculars from the glove compartment. The binoculars allowed him to scan the trails and roads running into the surrounding countryside. Then he went back to the cruiser again and grabbed his map of Ghost Ranch.

"Okay, here's a plan," Fernando said, looking at the map. "On the south side of the campground there's another road, a direct route to the Welcome Center. A couple of hundred feet down that road is a utility building. From there we could see the entire campground and all the paths leading in and out, from any direction."

Hank raised his hand. "So what are you suggesting?"

"Well, if the Ryan boys are hiding in the hills out there, at some point they'll likely come in to use the facilities or maybe buy food and water at the Cantina, right? So why don't we park the cruiser behind that utility building and watch the campground with our binoculars. If they show up, we move quickly before they have time to get their weapons out of the pickup."

"Okay, but what if they don't show up before nightfall?" Hank asked.

Fernando shrugged. "Then we rent a casita for the night and come back tomorrow morning?"

Hank shook his head. "Goddamn Ryans! I need to get back to Taos. I can't spend all day and all night here."

"What's the alternative?" Fernando asked.

Fernando waited while Hank considered.

"Okay, then let's do it," Hank said finally. "I just hope to hell we don't have to do this again tomorrow." With that, he climbed into the cruiser and slammed the door in disgust.

Hank drove to the road on the south side of the campground and down to the nearby utility building. He pulled into the parking lot behind the building, out of sight from the campground. They climbed out of the cruiser and explored the grounds. To the west Arroyo del Yeso ran alongside the building, separated by a thick patch of piñon and juniper trees. In the trees they found a rock formation that allowed one of them to climb to the top and sit on a flat stone surface. Only one. The other would have to wait at the bottom or back in the cruiser.

Fernando climbed the rock formation with his binoculars and scanned the campground. "Yep, I can see everything from here."

"Okay, let's take one-hour shifts," Hank said. "You first. Since you're already up there. I'll just twiddle my thumbs down here or whatever a person is supposed to do while he waits."

So they ticked off the hours, first Fernando and then Hank and then Fernando again. As dusk approached they were tired, bored, and hungry.

"Wait!" Fernando shouted finally, looking through the binoculars. "I see someone coming up from the arroyo north of the campground. He's getting closer. Looks like a fair-haired young man...I'm sure it's Donnie!"

"Is he armed?" Hank asked, straining to see Donnie with his naked eyes.

"No. And he's alone."

"Okay, but if we jump him now, Cowboy Jack might get away," Hank said. "Better to follow him to the camp and grab them both. Grab'em before they can get their guns and start shooting."

"He's going into the bath house now."

They waited several minutes, Hank pacing around the arroyo.

"Here he comes," Fernando said. "He's headed back to the arroyo. Back to their camp."

"Well damn, you know I'd tail him if I could," Hank said, dragging his bad foot and exaggerating his limp. "But with this bad foot...."

"I know, I know," Fernando said, climbing down from the rock formation. "I'm taking the binoculars with me. I'll find the camp and then come back for you. We'll take the cruiser down, see how close we can get."

Hank nodded. "You know I'd go if it wasn't for this foot."

"Un-huh. Last time I recall it was the arthritis in your knee," Fernando said. He tucked the binoculars strap around his shoulder and took off jogging toward the bathhouse.

21

Fernando reached the bathhouse out of breath. He stopped to check on Donnie's whereabouts. He spotted the younger Ryan brother halfway down the hill walking toward the arroyo. He followed at a distance, jogging from one piñon tree to the next. At the bottom of the hill Donnie disappeared into the arroyo, so Fernando cut over to the arroyo to follow him there. So far Cowboy Jack was nowhere in sight.

The sandy bottom of the arroyo slowed him down. His feet kept sinking in the soft sand. Overhead the sky had darkened. The further he walked the more the shadows deepened in the arroyo. Objects in his field of vision seemed to lose their edge, go fuzzy before his eyes. Finally he thought he heard muffled voices, so he stopped to listen. Nothing. He crept ahead, moving to the side of the arroyo and hiding in the shadows. Soon the arroyo turned sharply to the east. He edged around the bend, scanning the banks of the arroyo.

Again he thought he heard mumbled voices.

Fernando stopped, hugging the side of the arroyo.

"What do you want?" came a disembodied voice from above.

Fernando froze. He looked around, desperately hunting for the source of the voice. In the shadows he saw the outline of a man standing on the opposite bank of the arroyo.

Cowboy Jack. Instead of his western hat, he wore a baseball cap pulled down over his forehead. He held a pistol in his bandaged right hand. The pistol was pointed at Fernando.

"Put the gun away," Fernando said. "Your mother told us where you were. She sent us to bring you back. Hank is waiting up at Ghost Ranch."

"You're a liar," Cowboy Jack said.

Fernando calculated his chances. Cowboy Jack's bandaged right hand and the deepening shadows in the arroyo would be to his advantage. That would have to be enough.

"Your mother came to the sheriff's office this morning–" Fernando began, to distract Cowboy. Then he dove to his side and rolled behind the bend, while Cowboy fired off a burst of bullets that thudded into the side of the arroyo and sprayed him with sand.

Fernando scrambled to his feet quickly. He ran back toward the campground, slogging through the sand until he came to a spot where tree roots had crumbled the bank of the arroyo. Using the exposed tree roots as handles, he climbed out of the arroyo into a stand of piñon trees. As soon as he was on his feet he took out his Smith & Wessen. What to do? He wanted to go back and get Hank, but he would be a sitting duck once he stepped out on the trail. Cowboy Jack could use him for target practice.

Cowboy Jack made the decision for him.

"He's in the trees, I heard him climb up the bank!' Cowboy Jack shouted to Donnie. "Bring your gun."

"No! Don't shoot anyone!" Donnie shouted.

Fernando crept through the trees and pushed aside a snarl of branches. He saw their camp. The red tent, folding chairs, and a gas camping stove placed on a cardboard box. They had parked their pickup in another stand of piñon trees and then covered the exposed areas of the truck with dried tumbleweed and dead tree branches. It would be invisible from above.

Donnie sat in one of the folding chairs, holding his head in his hands and rocking back and forth. He appeared to be bawling like a baby.

"CRACK!" a bullet zinged through the branches above Fernando.

Cowboy Jack had spotted him.

Fernando moved back in the trees, away from the opening. "I don't want to shoot you. Drop the gun and come out with your hands up," he ordered.

"I'm not going back!" Cowboy Jack shouted and fired off another round.

This time the bullet thudded into a tree trunk beside Fernando.

Fernando moved further back in the trees. Behind him the path up to the campground had begun to disappear in the creeping shadows. If he waited fifteen or twenty minutes the hill would be totally dark and he could reach Hank safely. He just had to last another fifteen or twenty minutes. You can do it, he told himself. Keep moving back. Keep him guessing.

Suddenly he saw bouncing lights coming down the hill behind him. As the vehicle approached he identified it as an ATV careening down the trail. Whoever was driving must have taken lessons from Hank, a notorious speedster.

Fernando darted out of the trees and waved at the ATV. The driver slammed on the brakes and the ATV skidded to a stop in a shower of sand. Hank was riding shotgun. Next to Hank sat big man with a bald head and mustache.

Hank jumped off the ATV. "What's happening? I heard gunshots and decided to come on down." He pointed to the driver, still sitting in the ATV. "That's Eric, he works security at Ghost Ranch."

Eric nodded.

"Cowboy Jack says he won't go back with us," Fernando said. "Just in case I didn't get the message, he started shooting."

Hank cursed. "Is Donnie with him?"

Fernando nodded. "He's sitting at their camp down by the arroyo bawling like a baby."

"Goddamned Cowboy Jack!" Hank cursed. "Someone needs to teach that little shit a lesson."

"Don't shoot him. Remember what Ruth said she'd do."

Hank ignored Fernando. Living up to his youthful nickname of Sundance, he whipped out his long nose Colt .45 and burst through the trees, totally exposed. "Jack? Goddamnit, come out here right now. I'm taking you back to Taos whether you like it or not. I've known you since you were a pup. Now let's go!"

"Don't come any closer, Hank, or I'll have to shoot," Cowboy Jack said, his voice coming out of the darkness somewhere on the far bank of the arroyo. "I'm not going back."

"The hell you aren't! If I don't bring you back, your mother will shoot me," Hank roared.

Eric climbed off the ATV and walked through the trees. He, too, had a pistol in his hand. "Can I help?"

"Who's that?" Cowboy Jack asked.

"Security guard at Ghost Ranch," Eric said. "You need to come out and do what the sheriff says."

Fernando couldn't hold back any longer. He stepped out of the trees and raised his hands. "Listen, there's too many guns here. Everyone put away your guns before someone gets hurt."

At that Cowboy fired a shot that clanked on the metal of the ATV and ricocheted off into the side of the hill.

Then all hell broke loose.

"You shot my ATV!" Eric shouted and started firing wildly into the darkness.

Hank dropped to one knee and fired a shot over toward the arroyo.

Fernando dove for cover, landing in the dirt. He tried to locate Cowboy Jack in the darkness but couldn't. He focused on where he thought Cowboy Jack's voice was coming from.

Then Eric apparently had second thoughts about helping and scrambled back in the trees for cover.

Donnie screamed, "Don't shoot, Jack! You'll just make things worse! Don't shoot!"

"Listen to your younger brother, Jack," Hank shouted. "You're in enough trouble now, you don't need any more. We can help you if you come back with us now. I give you my word."

"No, I don't trust you!" Cowboy Jack shouted and fired again, this time kicking up sand next to Hank.

Hank shouted something, maybe to Cowboy Jack or maybe to one of the others, it was impossible to tell. Then he jumped up firing his Colt .45. Like a big bear bursting out of the forest he thundered through the tree branches shooting toward Cowboy Jack. The blasts exploded the lip of the arroyo across the way and sent Cowboy Jack pitching forward. They heard a thud when Cowboy Jack landed on the floor of the arroyo, moaning.

"Fuck! You shot him," Fernando said. He re-holstered his Smith & Wessen and climbed, half sliding down into the arroyo. He landed on his feet and looked around, spotting Cowboy Jack a ways up the arroyo. Then he ran over to Cowboy Jack, who lay face down in the sand.

Fernando rolled Cowboy Jack face up. He didn't see any blood or an obvious wound. "Where are you hit?"

Cowboy Jack struggled to breathe. He'd had the wind knocked out of him. He seemed unable to speak, holding his chest tightly and clenching his teeth. Gasping for air, he said, "What? No! Get off me!"

Fernando took the hint and rose to his feet. When he spotted Cowboy Jack's pistol in the center of the arroyo, he grabbed it and emptied the shells. Then he tossed the gun as far down the arroyo as he could.

Fernando noticed Donnie approaching the lip of the arroyo. Was the kid armed? He didn't appear to be carrying a gun.

Donnie stared at his brother. "Oh, no! Jesus! Is he okay?"

"I think so, I don't see a wound," Fernando said. "I think he just had the wind knocked out of him when he fell."

By then Hank and Eric had climbed down into the arroyo. "Did I wing him?" Hank asked, limping over to Cowboy Jack, who was now sitting up and rubbing his chest.

Fernando shook his head. "Don't think so. Looks like you shot the ground out from under him."

Hank turned to Cowboy Jack. "Damn it, Jack Junior, why'd you have to go and make this so hard. All we're trying to do is bring you back safe and sound so you can have your day in court and clear your name."

Cowboy Jack didn't answer. He seemed to have recovered, glaring at the three men standing over him. Angry.

"Can you hear me?" Hank asked.

"Yes, I can hear you. Do you think I'm deaf?"

Hank ignored Cowboy's Jack's attitude. "So here's what's going to happen. We'll book you and release you on your own cognizance. I'll take the file to the District Attorney. If he thinks there's enough evidence he may charge you with killing Armando. If he does, then your attorney will argue the shooting was self-defense in the context of an ongoing feud and that there's no definitive physical evidence to convict you. Easy peasy. At that point the District Attorney will likely drop the charges. If he doesn't, your attorney will ask for a summary judgment for the defense, meaning you. Either way you'll walk. Understand?"

"Then why go through with all this if it's already a done deal?" Cowboy asked. "Why the charade?"

"Because the District Attorney will summons all parties, the Ryans and the Luceros, and tell them in no uncertain terms that if one more person or head of livestock is killed, he will throw the book at the perpetrator, if not the whole lot of you."

Cowboy Jack said nothing.

"Right now your mama's hiring a hot-shot lawyer from Santa Fe, Raoul Garcia," Hank continued. "That should help with this other potential charge, the killing of Anne Lewis, which could be more serious."

"Wait a minute, I didn't have anything to do with the murder of Anne Lewis," Cowboy Jack shot back. "I told you I wasn't even with her that night. I for damn sure didn't kill her."

Hank frowned. "Then who did?"

The question lingered in the air for several awkward seconds.

Finally Cowboy Jack turned his head and looked at Donnie. He kept on staring at his younger brother until Donnie spoke.

"Me! I killed her, but it was an accident!" Donnie blurted out.

Everyone turned to look at Donnie.

Donnie started bawling again, weeping and wailing at the same time. "I didn't mean to, I swear I didn't. She made fun of me. I just wanted to show her."

Hank raised his hands. "Okay. Stop. Slow down and tell me exactly what happened. From the beginning."

Cowboy Jack spoke first. "See, I've been taking Donnie with me to the Sagebrush for hook-ups. To give him some experience with women. Sometimes I would bring him into the room with me. Other times he would come in later, after I finished."

Hank was nonplussed. "To give him some experience?"

"Yeah...he'd never been with a woman before this summer."

"So what happened that night?" Hank asked, turning to Donnie.

Donnie looked down, avoiding their eyes. "Well, the night before Jack had hooked up with Anne. He brought me into the bedroom after he finished. She was pretty drunk, saying all kind of mean things. We had sex, but I was too fast and she laughed at me. She made fun of me and said I didn't know how to satisfy a real woman like herself. Mean stuff, like that."

"And that's why you killed her?" Fernando asked. "Is that what you're trying to say?"

"No, I'm just telling you what happened," Donnie said, pleading with them to listen. "So the next night I wanted a second chance. I wanted to show her I could satisfy a woman. On my way to her room I saw her jump into the pool in the courtyard, so I quick went out by the diving board and took off my clothes. It was dark and she was busy swimming, so she didn't see me get into the water. I wanted to surprise her. You know, show her how good I could be as a lover. I swam after her and grabbed her from behind. I managed to take off her top, but she was kicking and struggling. I don't think she even knew it was me that wanted her. I tried to kiss her but she went limp, her body and all. She just slumped away in the water without moving. I was scared. I knew I'd be blamed for what happened, even though she was the one that fought me. So I left her in the water. I got dressed and ran out the back gate."

All eyes were on Donnie now. None of them spoke.

"So you see, it was an accident," Donnie pleaded. "I didn't mean to hurt her. That's the truth."

Finally Hank had heard enough. The big man shook his head and flapped his arms in the air. "Jesus Christ! Your feud with the Luceros was bad enough, but this...this is fucking unbelievable. How are you going to explain all that to your mama, never mind a judge? I could just...the two of you...." Hank trailed off, turning to Fernando as if asking for help.

All eyes turned to Fernando

"Yeah, but you're forgetting one thing--the kid's a juvenile," Fernando said calmly, trying to pacify Hank. "Anne Lewis had sex with a juvenile. Raoul Garcia will have a field day with this. He'll argue her drowning was an accident brought on by her reckless behavior with a juvenile. He knows damn well a Taos jury--and judge--will believe a local teenager over an older woman of questionable repute from Los Angeles. Fair or not."

"That may be," Hank said, turning to the Ryan brothers, "but you boys will still have to settle with your mama. Not even Raoul Garcia can help you with that."

Fernando laughed, sort of. Neither of the Ryan brothers laughed.

"Okay, let's get a move on," Hank said. "It'll be dark soon. Jack, you ride with me and Eric in the ATV, where I can keep an eye on you. Fernando, you and Donnie throw all their camping gear in the back of the Dodge Ram and meet us at the cruiser, up behind the utility building. You two can follow Jack and I back to Taos. Go right to the station."

Cowboy Jack grumbled something.

"Or, if you prefer, I can put the cuffs on you two Romeos and throw you in the back of the cruiser," Hank said. "We can just leave the damn pickup here to rot. Your choice."

Neither Cowboy Jack nor Donnie said a word.

22

On a morning two weeks later Fernando sat at his desk, back to his usual routine. He'd worked in his garden and puttered around his small adobe on Acequia Madre all morning and then driven to his office on Canyon Road to while away the afternoon. Since returning from Taos he hadn't received any legitimate calls or messages from potential clients wanting the services of a private investigator. Only Cyrus Applethorpe, an eccentric old crank from East Alameda Street, who asked him to help find an R.C. Gorman painting he'd lost track of, maybe sold or given away, he couldn't remember because he drinks a bit. Fernando reminded him that his ex-wife had been awarded the painting in their divorce settlement. Cyrus responded by telling Fernando to piss off and then went off on a long rant about cops being as useless as tits on a boar. Old Cy ended by quoting the bard on Fernando: "You pizzle!"

Truth be told, the downtime suited Fernando. He'd had enough excitement in Taos to last a while. Gave him more time to relax and take care of himself for a change. The knot on his head he'd received at the Sagebrush courtesy of Joe Monroe still hadn't disappeared entirely. Estelle wanted him to get a CT-Scan to make sure the wound wasn't serious, but he declined. He'd had several CT-Scans in the past after various accidents or beat-downs, every one showing less white matter than the last. At this point in his life he didn't care to know about any further deterioration. No thank you.

This morning he had his feet up on his desk reading the *Independent* when he heard a vehicle pull into the parking out front between Ruby's gallery and Essentia, the sex shop. That usually meant another client needed his assistance with a nasty divorce or something more dire. Sure enough, moments later he saw a big black shadow approaching his office door. Not liking the size of the shadow outside, he opened the top drawer of his desk and readied his Smith & Wessen. The shadow banged hard on the door and then opened it roughly, not bothering to wait for an invitation. Fernando smiled when he saw the black Stetson.

In walked none other than Taos County Sheriff Hank Mathews. The big man wore civvies today, jeans and a blue flannel shirt complemented by a bolo tie and a big grin on his hangdog face.

"So this is where you hang out," Hank said. "Not bad."

Fernando laughed. "It used to be an old garage. A friend lets me use it rent free."

Hank shuffled over to the desk and sat down on nearby chair. He still limped, but not as badly.

"Where's the uniform?" Fernando asked.

"It's gone!" Hank said. "After thirty years, I've had enough. I said the hell with it and retired. I'm on my way to Tucson to visit my son. He wants me to move there so he can look after me. Hah! That'd be a switch."

Fernando didn't hide his surprise. "No kidding? Who's minding the store up in Taos?"

"They brought in Chris Perez, a deputy from Mora County, temporarily," Hank said. "He's a good man. I think they'll make him permanent."

"So what triggered your decision, if you don't mind me asking?"

"It's just time to hang up the spurs," Hank said. "I been thinking about retiring for a while now, but this last craziness with the Ryans and Luceros--shooting each other over a ridiculous grudge with no legal consequences for any of them--that was the last straw."

Fernando nodded. "I can understand that. Kind of sours you on the profession."

Hank leaned back in his chair and stretched out his long legs. "Yes it does, big time. The profession ain't what it used to be. When we started in law enforcement, it was easy. You just threw the bad guys in jail and let the prosecutors and judges sentence them. Now you have to fight with the District Attorney and the judges over every goddamned person you arrest. The District Attorney's overworked. If he does file charges, he just wants to get the accused to sign off on a plea deal. If he can't get a plea deal, he's likely to drop the charges altogether. The judges are just as overworked. They want plea deals just as bad so they don't have to go to trial. And then they give light sentences to cut down on appeals. So what's the use of arresting the bad guys in the first place? No, it just ain't like it used to be."

Fernando nodded his assent. "Is that what happened with Cowboy Jack and Donnie?"

"Pretty much," Hank said. "The District Attorney dropped charges on Cowboy Jack for lack of evidence. No way to prove shooting Armando wasn't self-defense. Didn't even bother to lecture the two families, so I had to do it, once again. As if they would listen to me now when they hadn't paid one damn bit of attention to me for the last year."

"Then you think the feud will continue?" Fernando asked.

Hank shook his head. "Hell if I know. My hope is that Cowboy Jack and Donnie are more interested in womanizing than shooting Luceros. And that Rosalia Lucero can keep brother Tony on the straight and narrow. So I don't know. Maybe this brush with the law will be a turning point."

"You would think," Fernando said.

Hank sighed. "Donnie's case is a damn sight more complicated. Forensics found his DNA on the second used condom discovered in Anne Lewis' room, which corroborated his story, sort of. Raoul Garcia is working on the District Attorney now for a plea deal. Looks like Donnie will likely get a few months in Juvenile and then probation. I have to say, old Raoul's as good as you said he was."

Fernando laughed. "He's a piece of work, but he's a damn good lawyer. If you want to see a guilty man walk, just call Raoul."

"He's the magic man, all right," Hank said.

"So I guess we won't be working together again," Fernando said. "Unless, that is, you want to throw in with me and open an office in Taos. We could call ourselves "Northern New Mexico Investigations." Or how about "Low Road to Taos Investigations."

"Yessir, I like that last one," Hank said. "That would give me an excuse to avoid moving to Tucson. Let me think about it for a time. If my son doesn't kidnap me in Tucson, I just might be interested."

"I hear Tucson's not a bad town."

Hank smiled. "No snow, anyway. I get tired of all the snow in Taos. I'm too old to be slipping and sliding around in that white stuff."

"Still, we'd make a helluva pair, you and I. We work well together."

"Damn right," Hank said, hoisting himself up out of the chair and heading for the door. "Low Road to Taos Investigations. I like that."

Fernando smiled. "Why take the high road when you can go low?"

"Yes sir, we know a little something about that," Hank said, and walked out into the bright sunshine on Canyon Road.

Readers Guide

1. From the very beginning of *Taos Vendetta* it's clear to the reader there is great discord in the movie crew staying at the Sagebrush Inn. Explain the conflicts.

2. Why does Taos County Sheriff Hank Mathews call Private Investigator Fernando Lopez and ask for his help?

3. When Lopez arrives at the Sagebrush where Hollywood actress Anne Lewis was murdered, he talks to Sheriff Mathews and Cassie Jenkins, a member of the film crew, about the primary suspects. Who are they?

4. Why does Sheriff Mathews get upset when he learns that Cowboy Jack, a young man who frequents the Sagebrush bar looking for hookups, is one of the leading suspects? Why is Cowboy Jack trouble?

5. Explain the feud between the Ryan and Lucero families? What's the status of the feud as the story begins?

6. Ted Fisher, the executive producer of the film shooting in Taos, quickly becomes one of the chief suspects. How does Fisher try to derail the investigation into Anne Lewis' murder?

7. Why do Lopez and Sheriff Mathews find the movie being filmed in Taos laughable?

8. How do Lopez and Cassie Jenkins end up as roommates?

9. Sheriff Mathews, with the help of Lopez, attempt to intervene in the feud between the Ryan and Lucero clans. Is it successful?

10. How does Lopez end up in the hospital?

11. Why does Cowboy Jack become the leading suspect in the Anne Lewis murder investigation?

12. How does Lopez finally get rid of Joe Monroe, Ted Fisher's bodyguard?

13. Sheriff Mathews suffers a gunshot wound in the course of the investigation. Who shoots him? Why?

14. When Cowboy Jack flees and attempts to go off-grid in an abandoned farmhouse outside Arroyo Seco, how does Lopez find him? What happens when Lopez and Mathews find Cowboy Jack?

15. How does Ruth Ryan, the matriarch of the Ryan family, finally enable Lopez and Sheriff Mathews to capture Cowboy Jack and Donnie, his younger brother?

16. Where are the two runaways finally cornered? What happens in the ensuing confrontation?

17. What is the shocking final revelation at the end of *Taos Vendetta*?

www.ingramcontent.com/pod-product-compliance
Lightning Source LLC
Chambersburg PA
CBHW010357310726
48979CB00006B/1071

* 9 7 8 1 6 3 2 9 3 6 9 1 2 *